MAR 29 '23

BO

THE SKY
WE SHARED

THE SKY
WE SHARED

SHIRLEY REVA VERNICK

CINCO PUNTOS PRESS

An Imprint of LEE & LOW BOOKS Inc.

New York

CINCO PUNTOS PRESS
an imprint of LEE & LOW BOOKS Inc.
95 Madison Avenue,
New York, NY 10016
leeandlow.com

Manufactured in the United States of America. Printed on paper from responsible sources.

Edited by Elise McMullen-Ciotti
Book design by Sheila Smallwood
Typesetting by ElfElm Publishing
Book production by The Kids at Our House

The text is set in Bembo MT Pro

10 9 8 7 6 5 4 3 2 1 First Edition

Cataloging-in-Publication Data is on file with the Library of Congress
Names: Vernick, Shirley Reva, author.
Title: The Sky We Shared / Shirley Reva Vernick.
Description: First edition. | New York, NY : Cinco Puntos Press, an imprint of Lee & Low Books Inc.,
[2022] | Audience: Grades 7-9. |
Summary: Set during WWII and told in alternating voices, Nellie, a young Oregonian and survivor of a
balloon bomb sent over by the Japanese, strives to understand how the war has torn her community apart
and created prejudice against Japanese-Americans, while across the ocean, as part of her nationalist duty,
Tamiko helps create the balloon bombs, but in her struggle to survive hunger and starvation, Tamiko
muddles her way through her anger against the United States for the war.
Identifiers: LCCN 2021004893 | ISBN 9781947627529 (cloth) | ISBN 9781947627536 (paperback) |
ISBN 9781947627543 (ebook)
Subjects: CYAC: World War, 1939-1945—United States—Fiction. | World War, 1939-1945—Japan—
Fiction. | Toleration—Fiction. | Friendship—Fiction. | Grief—Fiction.
Classification: LCC PZ7.V5974 Fall 2022 | DDC [Fic]—dc23
LC record available at https://lccn.loc.gov/2021004893

FOR MIKIO, ESTHER, AND MARK TAJIMA

1

NELLIE DOUD

April 29, 1945
Bly, Oregon

I lie on my back in the front yard, spyglass in hand. Not that I'm spying on anyone. Why would I want to look into someone's window when I can look at the whole universe? Besides, everyone has their blackout shades pulled.

I squint into the eyepiece and pick out the Big and Little Dippers, the Lion, Hydra, the Twins—I always start with the constellations—then turn to the gibbous moon and the Dog Star. It's late but it's a clear, warm night, the downy grass soft on my neck, the scent of lilacs and charcoal in the air, crickets chirping. A bullfrog croaks. I could stay right here all night, even if Mother does say it's an unseemly thing for a girl going on fifteen years old to do.

My pa taught me about the sky. He'd be stretched out right alongside me tonight if he weren't in the service. The army has him posted in the Aleutian Islands, which I'd never heard of before, but now I know they're part of Alaska. I worry about

Pa up there, but not as much as I used to. After all, we routed the Japanese from the Aleutians two whole years ago. Now the posters say Alaska is a "death trap for the Jap." Good.

No, I'm not as worried anymore, but I miss him as much as ever. Maybe more than ever. Of all the people in my family, he's my person, my kindred soul. He's the one who loves the sky as much as I do, who I can tell my secrets to, who makes this house, this town, feel like home. The Aleutians might need him now, but that's not where he belongs, not really.

A movement low in the sky catches my eye. I turn my glass in that direction. Something is there, all right. It's darting, dropping, white and round. A falling star! Like a fairy light in a twinkling sky. I wish Pa were here to watch it with me. He'd know how magical it is.

Just as it shoots out of sight, a big furry dog knocks the spyglass out of my hand and slurps my face. Joey Cooper's dog!

"Hello, Poppy." I sit up and scratch behind her long ears. "You must like the lemon ice on my lips."

Across the street, a screen door screeches open and someone—it has to be Joey—steps out and whistles. Joey Cooper, the boy who's a year ahead of me, one dirt road across from me, and a world away.

It wasn't always that way. We used to be friends, really good friends. Best friends, as a matter of fact. I used to hope it might turn into something more than that, but then the war pulled Joey away from me. Him and Pa both.

He puts his fingers in his mouth to whistle.

"She's right here." I stand up but keep a tight hold on her.

Come talk to me, Joey.

"C'mon, girl," he calls a couple of times. She doesn't come, so he heads past the white oak in his yard, down his dirt driveway, across the road to where I stand.

I let go of Poppy's collar at the last minute.

"Hey, Nellie. Guess I got the dumbest mutt in town." In the moon's glow, his gray eyes are silver, his sandy hair gold.

"She's a good dog." I finger-comb my dark bangs. "I didn't see you at school today."

"Yeah, I had to help my uncle with the cows again." He pats Poppy's flank. "Tomorrow too. And Saturday."

The old Joey would laugh off the extra work. He'd say that there's no *udder* place quite like a farm, or something like that. He'd have me laughing too. But this Joey sounds sad. He's been sad for months now, ever since Bly got a new star, its very own. Not a winking white star in the sky. A cloth one, yellow, hanging in the Coopers' front window, letting everyone know that Joey's brother Peter was killed in action.

It happened in December. December was already dark in Bly. The blackout meant no outdoor Christmas lights. Rationing meant not enough sugar or butter for baking cookies, and no metal or rubber for children's toy airplanes and cars. That wasn't so bad. The real darkness was the terrible word about Hitler's surprise attacks in Europe, how fast the Nazis were advancing, how many of our soldiers died, including Peter Cooper. Killed in action. Gone forever.

I knocked on the Coopers' door as soon as I heard the news. No one answered. Mother said I should give Joey some time, but

Joey needed me. Or so I thought. We were best friends, after all. I tried again the next day—same thing.

Three days after the Coopers' star appeared, Mother and I brought over a pie. We had to use potato flour, so it wasn't very good. Joey was the one who answered our knock. He wore his brother's high school ring, gold with a blue jewel, along with the sorriest face I'd ever seen.

Before I had a chance to say a word, he disappeared up the stairs, calling out, "More visitors, Ma."

Mother and I went into the kitchen to find Mrs. Cooper slumped at the table and Poppy crouched underneath it. Mr. Cooper was milling around too. They discharged him from the army when the bad news came, because how much loss can one family take? Anyway, Mother offered "deepest condolences" and murmured, "He was a fine young man," and Mrs. Cooper whispered back, "No funeral plans yet—we're still hoping for Peter's . . . remains." After that, it was just silence.

What was Joey doing up in his room? What was he thinking about, and why wouldn't he come down and talk to me? I had no idea then, none now. Since then, he just goes to school—early, because he has flag duty—and works for his uncle. No more hanging around. No more jokes. No more talking.

"You gonna be at the salvage drive Saturday?" Joey asks me out of nowhere, straddling Poppy. Joey works on all of Bly's war effort projects, like helping run the fat collection station and picking milkweed pods to fill life jackets. We may only be a thousand strong in this one-blink town, but we do our part.

"Mm-hmm," I answer. "I'll be there."

"Me too." This is the most he's said to me in all these months, the closest he has stood.

"Mrs. Flynn is donating the bumpers off her car," I say. "She says it takes eighteen tons of metal to build one tank." I bite my lip, wishing I could take my words back—because for all anyone knows, Peter died in a tank. "You working metals this time, or rubber?"

He shrugs, presses his lips together. "Wherever they need me. How about you?"

"Yeah. Wherever they tell me."

Neither of us says anything.

"Guess I'll see you then," he says at last. "C'mon, Pops, time to head in."

"Yeah. Bye."

They go back across the dirt road, up the rutted driveway, into their house. It's a start, I guess. We talked a little. We'll see each other Saturday. That's something, anyway.

When I hear Joey's screen door slam shut, I lie back down in the tall grass and look up at the sky, hoping another star will fall. But none appears—and Joey doesn't ask me to hold his hand, and Pa doesn't come striding down the street. I fall asleep right there in the grass, who knows for how long.

I wake to the sound of Joey's door squeaking open, only this time it doesn't bang shut. He's changed out of his white T-shirt into a black turtleneck. He walks fast down his driveway and up the road. Where is he going in such a hurry? Is he in some sort of trouble? Does he have a girlfriend?

He passes my yard and the yard next door. Six months ago, I

wouldn't have to wonder where Joey was going. He'd have told me. He'd have asked me to go with him.

I jump up, shoving my spyglass in my trouser pocket and trailing behind him. Walking on the grass so he can't hear the sound of my feet, I follow him past half a dozen small houses and their oversize yards. Just past my friend Ruby's, we make a right-hand turn onto Hitching Post Lane, where Fish Hole Creek burbles its song. My heart sinks when he turns left onto hilly Upland Way.

Upland is a little dead-end street with only three houses on it, and one of them belongs to Irene Kava, who sits next to me in school. I can't stand Irene for a whole bunch of reasons. For one thing, she's stuck-up. Her father is head of the logging works, and she thinks she's better than everyone because she lives in a bigger house and has more stuff. For another thing, she's as mean as they come. She once said something so awful to me that I can't repeat it, and when Ruby overheard, she thought it was funny, so I had to be mad at her for a while too.

But the biggest reason I hate Irene is that her father had scarlet fever when he was young, and it left him with a weak heart. Which may not sound like a very good reason to hate someone, but it means her father will never get sent to war. He volunteers with the draft board instead, sitting behind a desk at the post office once every couple of months, signing up volunteers. Irene never has to worry about him getting shot or blown up or taken prisoner.

Joey turns into Irene's driveway. "Noooo!" I mutter to myself. Irene can't be Joey's girlfriend.

I sneak forward, hide behind the hedges close by. He looks at the darkened house, glances up and down the street, pulls something out of his pocket. Did he bring her a gift? Is she going to sneak out for a midnight stroll with Joey Cooper? Will she have on a sparkly new bracelet or necklace when she gets back home? Well, I'm not going to stick around to find out.

I can't leave yet, though. I'm too close—he might see me. I'll have to wait until Irene comes down. But Irene doesn't come down. After a few minutes, Joey heads up the driveway. He goes right past the house into the metal shed that stands off to the side. Is that where they're meeting? Is she already in there, waiting for him?

I want to escape—but I'm like a moth spiraling into a hot lightbulb. If I hear Irene giggling in there, I'm going to throw up.

Irene doesn't giggle. She doesn't make a peep. All I hear is . . . Well, I don't know what it is. It sounds like scratching. Then it's silent. Then more scratching. Then Joey comes out. Alone. He just stands there, facing the shed. More scratching.

And then I see it.

Fire! Flames creep from the back shed wall toward the front, getting fatter and brighter as they spread, like an advancing army.

Joey stares at the blaze, transfixed. It bewitches me, too, how the flames dart and twirl, crackling like Saturday-night popcorn on the stove, only louder. I can't take my eyes off the fire . . . until I notice Mr. Kava marching across his front yard in his bathrobe and pajamas, carrying a baseball bat. Or maybe it's a cane.

His bald head and ruddy face shine in the moonlight. He's on the short side, but he's broad and ramrod straight, looking more like a drill sergeant than the manager at the logging works. Could that be a rifle he's carrying?

Joey is still hypnotized. Mr. Kava is about to turn the corner around his house. He's going to see the shed, the fire—and Joey. Standing up, I pull my spyglass out of my pocket and throw it hard on the driveway. It clanks against the pavement and rolls away. I crouch back down.

Joey jerks to attention. "Wha—?"

He bolts, sprinting past the shed into the Kavas' backyard. I squeeze my eyes shut. *Stick to the fields, Joey. Don't stop running until you're back at your house.*

I never should have closed my eyes, though, never should have taken them off Mr. Kava. The next thing I know, he pulls me up by my shirt collar and stands over me with his baseball bat and his furious eyes, grumbling, "A girl?" Then he grabs my arm and drags me across his driveway, past the shed, over to his front steps.

2

TAMIKO NAKAOKA

September 15, 1944
Shinji-cho village, near Kure City, Japan

Ancestors,

It's a warm September afternoon in Shinji-cho. I feel you in the breeze as I walk home from school. The little boys on our crooked little road race around me, giggling and squealing, pretending to be fighter planes, their arms outstretched and heads bent. But still I can hear you in the wind—parents, grandparents, and all those who came before you, whispering welcome for my return.

The summer was long, now that summers are for working and not for resting. My older brother, Kyo, and I were sent to the rice paddies in the countryside to harvest food for our soldiers. It was difficult work, hunched over the rice stalks under the hot sun, but it had its good points. Well, it had one good point: We ate better than we do here.

Food is scarce here in Shinji-cho. The enemy is cutting off our shipments. What does get to our islands must go to our soldiers, of course. Still, even though our village has grown lean,

I'm glad to be back home, out of the sweltering sun and onto my own futon.

To tell the truth, though, I'm already weary of school. Eguchi-sensei is a clever teacher, but really, what use do I have for biology, geography, and history classes? I weave these subjects right into my embroidery—red-crowned crane, snowy Mount Fuji, emerald sea dragon, sparkling butterfly.

Needle and thread are all I'm good at, all I'll ever be good at. I'm almost fifteen now, after all. I don't think I'll wake up one morning and suddenly be a math whiz or a scientist. I wish I could be somewhere embroidering all day long. The theater perhaps. Yes, the theater, all costumes and spotlights and magic.

Last term, our class went to the Fantaji Theater in Kure City to see a play filled with ghosts, samurai, fair maidens, and demons. I fell in love with the dancing, the music, the incredible makeup, and the costumes. Especially the costumes. The theater! If I could bring my friend Suki with me so I wouldn't get lonely, and if you'd come with me, ancestors, I'd move to the theater in an instant.

Shizue-san, my aunt, tells me to be careful what I wish for. But it's a small wish—a sapling, not a tree—that will never come true anyway. Just a little wish—a raindrop, not a typhoon—with no hope of happening. Not now, anyway, not during war, and it's such a long war. But someday perhaps luck will take me there, to the costume room, to the spotlights and the magic, where I hope to bring you pride.

~ Tamiko

When I hear the front door open, I quickly make the character for the dragon and slide my diary into my dresser drawer. Kyo is late getting home from the war rally tonight, so late that Shizue-san is already snoring on her futon.

"I am home, sister," he says. Then he goes straight to his room to drop off his rucksack, while I get his bowl of moldy gray rice ready.

Kyo takes his place at the low table in the living room. His hair is windblown, his sharp cheekbones flushed. People say we look alike. I didn't see it before—he was always lanky and I was always plump. He always moved gracefully, like a cat, and I always limped and clomped from my bout with polio. But now that we're both gaunt from hunger, now that my cheekbones show too, now that I've cropped my hair, I must agree. We're visibly family.

I put the bowl in front of him. "This is all we have. Again. Grayer than ever."

"Hunger is the best spice," he tells me, but that's only a saying he has learned to parrot. There's also a saying that you should eat until you're eight out of ten parts full. That won't be happening tonight.

While Kyo digs into the rice, I sit down opposite him, and that's when I see. I see that he's hungry for more than food. It's right there in his eyes, the way they flash like swords. It's there in his chopsticks, the way they click like boot steps. Soon he'll be old enough to join the Imperial Army, and it makes me afraid.

"The rally, it started late?" I ask.

He shakes his head. "It ran long. Then I stayed after to talk to some of the soldiers. They're doing so much. They need everyone's support. Here." He pulls a pamphlet out of his pocket and hands it to me.

I flip through it, my eyes catching on White Westerners, arrogant colonists, evil greedy Allies, American atrocities. I know all this already.

"Kyo, what will you do? We need you, Shizue-san Auntie and I."

"I know," he says, solemn as a spider. "I mean to protect you. And I will."

"But we need you at our table, not in a foxhole. Not in an urn like poor Isamu across the street."

I know we must all sacrifice for the war effort, for our divine Emperor, for our homeland. That's why I go uncomplaining without food, without new clothes, without summers off. But must I sacrifice Kyo?

He takes the last bit of rice into his chopsticks. "Go to sleep now, Tamiko. I'm here tonight." Then he yawns and goes to his room.

My sweet, hardheaded brother doesn't really hear me, not tonight, not last night, not the night before. His head has been too full of stars, ever since the fellow from the Tsuchiura air base visited our school last month. The soldier looked very smart, dressed in his crisp uniform and standing at attention. As we gathered on the dusty school grounds, I felt ashamed of our plain school uniforms. I felt embarrassed by our school, which looks more like an oversize house than the proper schools of the city.

He didn't seem to mind our homeliness, though. His eyes

were glued to the skies as he told us about his training to be a kamikaze pilot. Soon he'll crash his plane into an enemy warship, giving his life for our Emperor, for our nation. He smiled when he told us how the kamikaze boys are all given a hachimaki—a kind of headband—made by a thousand women. On each hachimaki is a rising sun, symbol of good fortune, to take with them to their most honorable death. He stood tall when he recited the pilot's oath. He looked content when he described the cherry blossoms they paint on the sides of their bombers, bright white flowers hemmed with palest pink. Was that how he truly felt?

As the pilot spoke, I thought of the cherry tree in front of our school, how it bursts into bloom each spring, how the fragile blossoms fall to the ground two weeks later. Soon, this soldier's splintered body will be scattered like petals in the wind. An honorable death, but a grisly one. I wondered if the kamikaze boys leave suicide notes. Then I thought of Kyo. How easily my brother could be wheedled into volunteering with them—the poor fool, like a fish in the net.

On the way home from school that same day, I told Suki I might take a needle and stitch Kyo to my side to keep him from joining the army. She shrugged her black pigtails, smiled that smirky smile of hers, and said, "At least he'd get fed in the service."

She's right, I suppose. Food is harder and harder to come by here. It's the American submarines, cutting off our shipping supplies.

Just yesterday, Auntie brought me an old blouse of hers. "Here," she said. "This dragon you embroidered on the sleeve.

Can you turn it into a koi fish? To make it look newer when we trade it." My aunt is wrinkled and stooped, her snowy hair a stranger to the glossy black of her youth, but she's sly. "Maybe not a koi. Maybe a maneki-neko cat."

I shook my head. That would be like applying eye drops from a second-floor balcony. "Come, Auntie," I said. "I will unravel the old threads and sew something from scratch. A dragonfly or a swallow, maybe a lucky frog. Your blouse will look like new then, and when we trade it, we can get something decent to eat."

"A little something sweet for you," she offered.

"A piece of fish for you," I said. "And white rice for Kyo." This is how we make do.

After washing Kyo's rice bowl tonight, I crawl onto my futon in the room I share with my aunt. I'm tired, but before I go to sleep, I speak to my parents' spirits. "Otoosan and Okaasan," I say. "If you can find your way to Kyo tonight and whisper in his ear, maybe he'll stay where he belongs. He will join you in the other world soon enough. Please let it not be now."

I worked all last evening on Auntie's blouse. I snipped out the dragon, frayed and dull, and embroidered a turtle in its place, using bright green thread to stand out against the black fabric. On the other sleeve, I made a swallow, long-legged and graceful.

Today I take the blouse to the old lady they call Pāru—Pearl, because of her big white teeth. She ran a flower shop in better times. Nowadays, she trades in whatever she can find—a pair of sandals, a half-pound of squid, a sweet potato. Everyone in the village knows to go to her cottage on the outskirts when they can't find what they need at a store, which is often. When I get there this afternoon, two women are ahead of me. They haggle and squabble with Pāru before exchanging their goods and heading home. I have to wait a long time.

"Konnichiwa—good afternoon," she says when it's finally my turn.

"Konnichiwa," I say, and we bow.

We're standing in front of her cottage. She conducts all her business out here, never letting customers inside, never allowing anyone to see her full stock. I wonder where she gets her goods. Some of it she gets from bartering with us villagers, yes. But where does she get the fish, the eggplant? Well, no matter. As long as she gets it.

"What have you today, Tamiko-san?" she asks.

"A lovely blouse." I unfold it and let it hang.

She comes closer and picks up one sleeve, squinting. I look at her cloudy eyes and her lined mouth, unable to tell what she's thinking.

"It's made of fine material," I venture.

"It was made before you were born," she answers, not harshly, just matter-of-factly. She examines the other sleeve, then the collar. "What are you looking for today?"

"A trout or sea bass, if you have it, and some white rice. Also, if you have any thread, or else some cloth."

She strokes her small chin and disappears into her house. Several minutes later, she returns with some squid meat, a sack of dried beans, and a single chinsuko cookie, a sort of shortbread.

I swallow hard. This isn't what I asked for. But it's better than going hungry, and I can share the cookie with Suki. Still, if I try bargaining with her like those women did, maybe I can get some real fish. I waver. Then Pāru pulls a small spool of thread from her trouser pocket and hands it to me. It's purple and shiny and like no color I own. It will make a lovely butterfly or wisteria flower. We have a deal.

3
NELLIE
April 30, 1945

"I know who you are." Standing over me on his front steps, Mr. Kava looks broader and fiercer than ever, almost ferocious. "You're the Doud girl."

He leans over a garden hose and turns on the spigot. Hose in one hand, baseball bat in the other, he marches toward the shed. "Stay put," he barks over his shoulder.

I obey. I want to run, but I need to beg for mercy. So while Mr. Kava douses the fire, I rack my brain for something to tell him. "Yes, I did it," I whisper, "but it was an accident. I was trying to light a cigarette. I dropped the lit match, and it took."

I'm cooked.

"Yes, I did it," I try again. "Your daughter Irene torments me horribly, you see. She drove me to it."

Roasted, baked, deep-fried.

Mr. Kava comes back a few minutes later, panting a little as he crosses the yard. Then he surprises me by sitting down on the steps right next to me. His flannel robe smells of the smoke. He wheezes as he exhales. Mr. Kava has a weak heart—it would be awful if he died right here, right now.

"Mr. Kava, I—"

"I know you didn't do it." His voice isn't nearly as gruff as before.

"You do?"

"Course I do." He scratches his bald head. "What I need to know is, who did? I need you to tell me who you were with."

"I wasn't with anyone, I swear." And it's the truth. I wasn't *with* Joey. I was following him.

"Come on now. What's your first name?"

"Nellie."

"Nellie, that's right. Bill Doud's girl. Look here, Nellie. I'll tell you what. You tell me who did this and I'll keep mum about you being the accomplice, how's that? You give me the name, and you walk scot-free."

"You're wrong, Mr. Kava. I did do it. I really did."

"Then tell me this, Nellie. Tell me why you threw this thing on the driveway." He pulls my spyglass from his bathrobe pocket and hands it over.

A wave of dizziness drenches me. "I don't know, sir. I just, I saw the fire and . . ."

"You saw the fire, eh? I thought you said you set the fire."

Poached, sautéed, filleted.

"I mean—"

"It was the Cooper boy, wasn't it?"

My chest clamps. "I don't . . . I . . ."

"You can stop pretending. I saw him poking around the

other night. Didn't know he was casing the joint. Can't say I blame him, really."

"You can't?"

"I like the boy, that's the funny thing."

"Everyone likes him."

"Hmm, guess I can be grateful he didn't try to burn the house down. Nothing but a few rusty garden tools in that shed, and tin walls to contain the flames. The boy's right, too."

I turn my head in the direction of the shed. "He . . . he is?"

"Not about setting things on fire." He yanks on his ear like he's trying to cast out a bad sound. "I never should've let his brother enlist. Hell, seventeen. Still all snips and snails and puppy-dog tails. A war is the last place Peter Cooper belonged."

A memory comes to me. Last fall. Joey and I were heading home from school, with Ruby and my younger twin brothers dragging behind. Joey was telling me how Peter had just signed up, and I could hardly believe it.

"Peter?" I marveled. "Peter's really going off to the war?"

"Yup. First to Camp White for training," Joey said. "Then off to fight."

"Where—Germany, Japan?"

"Don't know. Could be anywhere."

"But he's not old enough," I pointed out.

"No, but Mr. Kava, he told Peter"—and here Joey put on a deep voice—"'Look, son, it's not so much that you're a few months shy of eighteen, it's that you're scrawny as a beanpole. I'll gladly take you on if you can get your weight up to minimum.'"

"How'd he do it?" I asked.

"Ate his weight in potatoes every night." Then, as if Joey could read the future, he added, "The fool."

Now, sitting here with Mr. Kava, smelling the scorched air, I see I missed it. All these months when Joey was looking nothing but sad, he was angry. Angry at Mr. Kava for enlisting Peter. Angry at Peter for choosing to leave. Angry at the war and the fighting and the killing. Maybe even angry at me for still having my brothers. That rage has been brewing under his skin all these months, brewing and festering and waiting for the right moment. For tonight. For the chance to light a fire in the enlistment man's shed.

Which makes Joey a fool, just like his brother who snuck into the war, like Mr. Kava who allowed it, like me for sticking my nose in it. Only, I can't really fault Joey. I could never fault Joey.

"Nope," Mr. Kava sighs, resting his elbows on the step above. "I never should've let that boy sign up."

"Then why did you?"

"Lots of reasons. No reason, really. Guess I figured, if I can't be there myself, I should send as many lads in my place as possible. Idiotic, eh?"

"I don't know." I tap my foot. "I hate those man-eating Nazis. And Japan, they attacked us first. So yeah, I want them destroyed too." I stop tapping. "I just . . . I don't know."

He takes a big breath and nods his head. "How'd he sucker you into being the lookout, anyway? Oh, it doesn't matter. I'll just have to hope he got it out of his system. You might as well be on your way."

I jump up. "You won't tell his folks?"

"Not as long as he stops."

I could kiss his shiny bald head. "Thanks, Mr. Kava. Thank you kindly." I wonder how he's going to explain the fire to Irene.

"Off with you then."

4

TAMIKO

October 1, 1944

Eguchi-sensei,

You've taught me many things in your classroom, and I've tried to grasp them all. Our principal has told me many things at our Morning Address assemblies, and I've listened hard. Here's something I understand and know to be true. Emperor Hirohito is a son of our goddess Amaterasu. He's now fighting a holy war. We, his servants, are a hundred million hearts beating as one.

Here's something I don't understand. We're told that our army is superior, that the weak Americans are panicked, that the gods are with us. But where is our final victory against the demons? Where is our peace? Where are all the things our great nation deserves?

You're a wise man, Eguchi-sensei, and perhaps you have the answers to all my questions. But I'll never ask them. I shouldn't even think them. Yet when I lie awake in bed or walk home from school, and especially when I'm in the middle of your math lessons, this is where my thoughts take me. Me, one of the hundred million hearts trying to beat as one.

~ Tamiko

My heart despairs, for today Kyo leaves to serve our Emperor. He looks happy as he prepares to go, his rucksack on his back, his trousers falling loose around his waist. I almost feel glad for him. I try, anyway. I try to catch some of the energy radiating off him, try to drink in that daring mood, but then I start to weep, and Auntie does too, because we know he might never return. And even if he does come home one day, he'll surely endure terrible things.

"Why must you go?" I ask him for the hundredth time.

"Because your stomach is shrunk to kumquat size."

"And my heart will shrivel like a pickled plum if you leave."

"Never mind your heart. You're hungry, Tamiko. We're all hungry. The enemy doesn't let us eat."

There's no denying this. The rice is as gray as mud. Squid is a delicacy. We haven't seen a fresh vegetable in ages. Every day the radio tells us how the Americans are cutting off our food. Why do they make us suffer like this? Our people would never do such a thing. We wouldn't starve anyone.

"I don't want you to die," I tell Kyo between sobs.

"Duty is heavy as a mountain; death is lighter than a feather." The words come from his mouth, but I know they're not from his own head. They're straight from the war rallies.

He's calm, calmer than I've ever seen him, as if a tranquil

spirit is sitting on his soul. As if he knows in the very pit of his being that this is the one right thing to do, the only thing to do. To fight the enemy that kills our people, chokes our food sources, sabotages our Emperor in his divine duty to unite the eight corners of the world. Kyo may be foolish and hardheaded, but of the hundred million hearts beating as one, none is truer than his.

He opens the cottage door.

"Please come home, Kyo."

He smiles softly. Bows. Grips his rucksack. And without another word, he runs off to meet the others in the town center. Auntie and I stand on the steps, waving. I try to see our narrow lane as he is seeing it, as someone who may never come here again. I try to feel the uneven road under my feet. Study the quaint wood-and-plaster cottages sandwiched against each other. Run my fingers over the morning glories that dot the way. Memorize each sight and sound. Swallow down my despair.

Kyo turns the corner. Long after Auntie goes back inside, I stay, watching.

Our grandmother once told us a tale about the Mirror of Matsuyama. In it, an ill woman gives her daughter a magical hand mirror moments before death comes. When the mother passes away, all the girl has to do is look into the mirror and she can see her mother in happier days. At least, that's how I remember it. Now as I stand on the steps trying to recall Kyo's gentle presence, I wish I had a magic mirror. I wish I could always see Kyo happy and well. Tears gather in my eyes again.

But then I smile. A small smile, just to myself. Kyo didn't notice, but I slipped one of my little Daruma dolls into his rucksack for good luck. He won't see it for a while, the red, egg-shaped thing with the bearded face and no eyes. I colored in one eye this morning and wished for his safe return. When he comes home, I'll color in the other eye. Please let that be soon, I beg all the spirits and ancestors.

When I go back inside, my aunt is at the altar in the sitting room, making an offering of salt to our household kami. She stands on tiptoe to reach the high shelf adorned with the kamidana box, the water jar, the little dishes of salt and raw rice, the evergreen branches, and the sacred mirror. She's probably already deep in worship, praying for my brother.

I want to give her some privacy, so I head to our room. There, I find a note Kyo left on my dresser.

Tamiko,

Soon you and Auntie will get used to not having me at home. That's good. Promise you won't forget me though. I'll think of you every day. With our ancestors looking over me, I'll return to you in triumph. That, little sister, is my greatest wish. Remember what our grandfather always said: "Even the wishes of an ant reach the heavens." Until then, take care of Auntie and don't fret about me.

~ Kyo

That's all, just a short note that punctures the storm cloud behind my eyes and sends the tears raining down again. I cry and cry because, for all of Kyo's reassuring words, I fear I'm holding his suicide note.

Auntie is old, but her hearing is young, and she can tell I'm weeping. She comes in and stands beside me, saying, "Fall down seven times, get up eight."

I don't—can't—respond.

"They get fed well in the army," she reminds me.

I nod. But it's cold comfort. I open my top dresser drawer and place Kyo's note inside.

"What is that?" Auntie asks.

"A note from Kyo." I reach to the back of the drawer and pull out the shiny purple thread from Pāru. "He wants me to embroider something to remind you of him."

"I don't need any reminders."

"I know." I squeeze her hand. "But it's what he wants. Bring me your scarf, and I'll get to work."

She lets go of my hand and steps heavily over to her own dresser. "Best make it a skinny boy with a head full of stars, then."

5
NELLIE
May 1, 1945

Mother and the twins are still asleep when I drag myself out of bed, exhausted from last night at the Kavas'. I make breakfast and lunch for Willie, Henry, and me. Same thing every day: two pieces of buttered toast apiece, plus a sandwich to carry to school.

Now that they've banned pre-sliced bread, I have to carve the loaf myself. They think we'll eat less bread this way—use less wheat and waxed paper—but really it just makes us fight over the thickest slice. The twins are annoying like that, acting like the eight-year-olds they are, always wanting what they want when they want it, no matter that there's a war going on.

I stand at the counter in our little kitchen with its white cabinets and yellow walls, watching the sunrise through the window, when my knife slips. I slice my finger instead of the bread. Ugh, there's blood. It makes me think of war, of all the soldiers. Of Joey's brother. Of Pa. Of those bloodthirsty Nazis and Japanese, and all the people they've killed trying to take over the world.

Please let Pa be all right. Please bring him home soon and in one piece. I'll do anything, I'll even try to be nicer to Henry and Willie.

Suddenly the twins are in the kitchen, clamoring for breakfast, their tawny curls unbrushed, their skinny legs sticking out from their shorts like jointed sticks. Mother is on their heels, getting ready for her part-time job at the post office now that Mr. Cokely, the postmaster, is in the service. She had her pick of jobs with so many of our men away now, but she wanted this one, the one where she gets to see people and keep tabs on them.

I press my cut finger against a dish towel and put the coffeepot on. I don't know how Mother drinks the stuff these days. Doesn't she notice how awful it is with no milk and half the usual sugar? Nope. She doesn't notice much of anything now that Pa is away, and whatever attention she does have goes straight to the twins and the post office. Sometimes I think the only thing Mother and I have in common, besides our brown eyes, is *Take It or Leave It* on the radio.

We all eat and wash up, and then the boys and I head out to pick up Ruby for the twenty-minute walk to school. I'm dying to tell her about last night, about Joey and the fire. Only I can't, I can't possibly tell her. Not because I don't trust her to keep a secret, but this is Joey's secret, not mine.

"Can we play with Ruby's pigeons?" Henry asks.

"They're not pigeons, they're doves," I say. "And they're not Ruby's. They're her grandpa's, like everything else in that house. Besides, we don't have time."

"Okay, okay. You don't need to get sore."

"And you don't need to be a pain in the neck." So much for me being nicer.

Ruby is lazing on her front stoop, a licorice lace in her hand, her brown-and-white saddle shoes tapping, her checked dress already too small to get her through another season. She tucks her strawberry locks over one shoulder and heads our way.

"Hey, Tweedledee and Tweedledum," she says to the twins. "Or are you both TweedleDUMB today?"

They laugh and run ahead of us, turning the corner onto the Big Road that connects Bly to the other villages. I'm sure the twins like Ruby better than me, on account of she's friendlier and jokier with them. Easy for her—she doesn't have to live with them.

"And hello to you too, Nellie Bly." That's her nickname for me ever since we learned about the world-traveling newspaper reporter in history class. "You look a little beat today."

"Couldn't sleep last night."

"How come?"

"Um . . ." I pull up my sock and rearrange my plaid skirt.

"Something on your mind?"

The twins have found a muddy makeshift baseball field next to a half-collapsed barn and are trotting around it—in their school shoes. "Get away from there!" I shout. "Mother will have your heads. Mine too." Then under my breath, I add, "You little beasts."

"Hey, Ruby," Henry pants, running our way. "Did you know girls play in the league now? In dresses and lipstick—it's the rule."

"What, no high heels?" Ruby tousles his hair, and he blushes because he's clobbered on her.

A car passes by. I look up just in time to see that it's Joey and his father. Joey's probably getting a ride to his uncle's farm. I wave, but Joey doesn't see me, like he's in another world.

"Y'know what I wish?" Willie pipes up. "I wish Joe DiMaggio didn't have to go and sign up. He belongs with the Yankees, not the army."

"The air force," Henry corrects him, standing up straighter. "Hey, Ruby, Willie and me are gonna play pro when we get older. Willie, wait up!"

"That's funny," Ruby says, sidestepping a pothole. "Just yesterday, Gramps asked me what I want to do when I'm older. Didn't even think of baseball."

"Well, what *do* you want to do when we get older?" I ask.

"Oh, I don't know. Get rich and see the world . . . if there's a world left to see, that is. You?"

"I'm gonna be a teacher, you know that."

"Yeah, but where?" She takes a bite of her licorice whip. "California, New York?"

"What's wrong with Oregon?"

She shakes her head and rolls her eyes. "I suppose next you'll say what's wrong with Bly."

"Well, what *is* wrong with Bly?"

"What's wrong with Bly?" She laughs that husky laugh of hers. "It's the size of a dried pea. It's boring. It's all we've ever known. Where's your spunk, Nellie Bly? Your sense of adventure?"

"Up there." I tilt my head up to the sky. I don't need to travel the world or even the country to see the stars and the planets. I've got them right here. With any luck, I'll have Pa back here before long too. Maybe even Joey.

"Anyway." Ruby shoves her licorice into her pocket. "As long as the war is over by the time we graduate, I'll be happy."

The end of the war. Soldier homecomings, ticker tape parades, the end of ration stamps and blackout shades. "Just think of it. All the butter and sugar we can eat."

"Cakes and pies and jam. And meat. Lots and lots of meat." I put my arm on her shoulder. "Let's cook ourselves a big fancy supper when it's official."

"A whole feast."

"Deal," I say.

Ten minutes later, we reach the white clapboard school-house, which looks sort of like an old church without a steeple. Even though I know Joey is doing farm work today, I find myself looking for him in the schoolyard, like I do every day. First I shoo the twins inside, then I glance around, a casual kind of look-see so no one can tell I'm scouting, no one will suspect I'm spying. Joey isn't there, of course. A minute later, when Ruby and I get to our mixed-grade classroom, Irene isn't here either, and I wonder if that has anything to do with last night. Well, at least I know Joey and Irene aren't missing school together. Joey hates that family. And I know exactly why—which is the way it's sup-posed to be with best friends . . . even if he doesn't remember that.

6

TAMIKO

October 7, 1944

Sweet Suki. She has decided we must go to our public shrine so I can pray for Kyo's good fortune. It's been almost one week since he left with his comrades. Six days, to be exact. Six days and six letters I've written to him at the Hiroshima training center. I picture him with his short-clipped hair and his baggy new uniform, learning how to use weapons, disciplining his body, caring little whether he meets an honorable victory or an honorable death. One week ago, he knew nothing of war except what he heard at the rallies. Now he's a soldier.

Since Suki lives on the other side of town from me—the nicer side—we agreed to meet in the village center, which is really just a short string of storefronts on an old dirt road. By the time I get there, my polio-damaged leg is hurting, up at the top, by my hip. I call it my fire-horse hip because that's how it feels, like a stallion with blazing hoofs is galloping across it. I'm used to it though, so it doesn't slow me down much.

I'm early, so I wander past the narrow two-story buildings, all painted white. I walk under their tile awnings for some shade, passing the coffeehouse, the boutique, the sake brewery, all closed now, their owners in their homes upstairs trying to figure out how to make ends meet. Ah, the tea and gift shop is still open for business. At least there's that.

"What are you shopping for?" asks Suki, suddenly at my side. She's panting as if she ran all the way here. She probably did—she has two strong legs, after all, and no fire-horse hip.

"The only thing I want isn't for sale—Kyo's safety," I say. "Let's go."

"All right." She glances over her shoulder. Her older sister and little brother are heading our way.

"Are we all going?" I ask.

"No, Fuyumi is getting Nori out of Mother's hair, that's all."

Fuyumi. Nori. Mother. Suki has her whole family. No one has died. No one has gone off to war—her brother is too young and her father is too old. No one even has a horse-fire hip. They all still live together in the house where she was born. I try not to envy her, but it's hard.

Just then, one of Kyo's friends comes out of the tea shop where we stand. He nods to us, then plants his gaze on Fuyumi, the beautiful Fuyumi with the large eyes and cherry mouth and swan neck. All the boys sneak looks at her, just as all the boys used to sneak looks at her mother.

Poor Suki. She takes after her father, with the long face and the large bones. Boys never stop to look at her. They don't stop to look at me either, but at least I don't have it rubbed in my face every day. I wonder if Suki envies me this one thing. No, probably not.

"Come on," I say again. "Let's go."

We walk past the shops, around the corner, to the small park where the shrine stands. "When were you here last?" I ask.

"Too long. You?"

"Same."

Several little boys run around the park, some of them playing tag, some of them pretending to be fighter planes. Their mothers sit on a bench nearby, watching and talking. The day is warm and cloudless, a good day for little boys to frolic. We skirt them and step through the shrine's wooden torii gate, stopping at the water fountain to wash our hands.

Suki pours a ladleful over her open palm. "The water is cold today."

"As long as it's fresh," I say.

She pours more water into her cupped hand and slurps it up. After rinsing her mouth, she spits it on the ground.

I take the ladle from her and do the same. The water feels like the winter to come.

We clasp our wet hands and walk up the stone steps, between the guardian lion dogs, into the shrine—a small open-air space made of plain wood with a bark roof. The crisp, mossy scent of cypress fills our nostrils as soon as we enter. It's like standing in a forest or inside a single living tree.

We pause to inhale the sacred feeling. No one else is here. It's only us and the powerful kami energy. Such a great force—but is it strength enough to keep my brother safe?

"Go ahead," Suki urges.

"Yes," I say, but don't move.

"Tamiko, did you forget your coin?"

"No, I have it." I reach into my pocket and pull out a ten-sen coin. Still, my feet stay put, so Suki links her arm through mine and leads me to the wooden offering box.

"Go ahead," she says. "For Kyo."

I nod, taking my strength from Suki. I need her more than ever now that Kyo is away. I wish I didn't, but I do. I toss my tin coin into the box and listen to the paltry plink it makes against the other coins inside. Stepping back, I bow two times, clap my hands twice, bow again, and say a silent prayer. *Please keep my brother alive. Please bring him home soon.* That's all.

"Did I do it right?" I ask Suki. I've been here many times, but now I can't remember how to pray.

"Exactly right."

"The coin felt heavy in my hand. Like a rock."

"Well, it flew like a butterfly." She takes my hand. "We're done now. Let's go outside."

The cool air feels good on my face as we walk between the guardian lion dogs, through the torii gate, to the grassy park where the little boys are still playing tag. After the hush of the shrine, I'm glad to be back in the daylight, the noise, the wide spaces.

"Let's sit here," I say when we reach an oak tree near where the mothers chat on their bench. I'm about to settle down when suddenly I jump back.

"Tamiko, what is it?"

"I heard something." My heart beats like a sparrow's wings.

Suki looks behind her and then up at the tree. "It's gone," I say.

She narrows her eyes at me, then tilts her head to listen. "Ah, I hear it now."

"You do?"

"Yes. It's the sound of Kyo laughing. He heard you had trouble lifting a ten-sen piece."

I fold my arms. "Suki."

"Wait, what's this?" She puts her hand to her ear. "He says he wants you to stop worrying so much." She smiles her smirkiest smile at me.

In this moment, it's hard to resent her for all she has. She's my best and wisest friend, and I cherish her. "Fine. I'll try." I sit down, and she joins me.

"What do you think Kyo is really doing right now?" she asks.

"Training, the poor fellow."

"Is it that bad?"

I swat a bug away. "The soldiers he met at the war rallies said they do marches, drills, and weapons practice all day long."

"Kyo isn't used to physical labor. And he's so skinny."

"He was looking forward to it, if you can believe. He said they learn to crawl on their bellies with fake bombs strapped to their backs."

"Why?"

"To practice slipping under the American tanks."

She shakes her head. "He must sleep like the dead at night."

"They do night training too. Full moon, no moon, they're out there."

Suki shakes her head again and gazes at the carefree little boys, standing in a circle for a new game. One of the bigger boys grabs a ball out of a smaller boy's hands.

"That's wrong," I say.

"Yes, that big boy should give the ball back."

"What? No, I mean Kyo." I straighten my legs out in front of me. "Working day and night for the war. And all we do here is sit. I wish we could do something. Something to help. To make a difference."

"Well, we came here," Suki says. "I think that's going to help. It's going to bring good luck to Kyo."

"He needs all the luck he can get. That's why I hid a Daruma doll in his rucksack."

"Ha!" she laughs. "How long do you think it took him to find it?"

"I hope he never finds it, or else he might toss it. I want it to stay right there with him."

"Do they let the soldiers keep their belongings?" she asks.

"I don't know. Probably not."

"Well, it doesn't matter." Suki pulls on her pigtail. "That Daruma doll has Kyo's name on it. Now you've done two things to help him."

"Do you really think so?"

"I know so."

Suddenly, two little boys come careening at us. We scoot away so they can use our tree to hide from each other. "Bang, bang!" one of them shouts. "I killed you!"

"You missed!" The other boy scampers off.

"I'll get you!" calls the first. "I'm pure, and you're the devil. Bang!"

"That's what Kyo is learning to do." I sigh.

"He's also learning how to keep himself safe." Suki stands up and offers me her hand. "Let's head back. I still have homework."

"Me too." I take her hand, and we head out of the park, leaving the little boys to romp, the mothers to visit, and the kami to look over us all.

7

NELLIE

May 1, 1945

All through the Pledge of Allegiance, I think about Joey and the fire and Mr. Kava. Mostly about Joey. I'm glad Irene isn't standing next to me this morning with her oh-so-lovely blond waves flowing down her oh-so-smart sweater set. Even if she's not Joey's secret sweetheart, I can't stand her, and I might be tempted to let slip that I know about her shed, which would lead to all kinds of trouble. Yup, best that she's tucked away at home.

When the pledge is done, Mrs. Flynn pulls out her announcement sheet. "'Remember,'" she reads, "'tomorrow is the community salvage drive here at the school. Families are asked to support the war effort by bringing in their scrap tin, rubber, and steel. Victory is near, so join the scrap by donating your scraps.' Any questions?"

A row ahead of me and three seats over, Joan Patzke raises her hand. Joan is as scrawny as a rail, with a dark ponytail and lots of freckles. She used to be friends with Ruby and me, but now we don't see much of her outside of school. Guess we just grew apart.

"Yes, Joan?" says Mrs. Flynn.

"So they won't be collecting paper this time?"

Mrs. Flynn double-checks the announcement sheet. "No, not this time."

Joan nods and turns around to look at her older brother, Dick. "Told you so," she mouths.

"Please take out your history books," Mrs. Flynn says.

Mrs. Flynn is bare-legged under her skirt because all the nylon has gone to make parachutes. The funny part is that she draws a fake seam up each calf with black ink, or maybe it's eyebrow pencil. I wonder if she ever hears the boys mumbling, "Mrs. Flynn is showing skin." Or if she sees their Green Lantern comics hiding inside their civics books. Or if she notices Ruby and me whispering all through math lessons.

I really don't think she pays any attention, not lately anyway. I think she's too busy worrying about her husband. He's an airman, and Mrs. Flynn used to bring in his letters to read out loud to us. There was the one about the newfangled chocolate buttons they were getting in their rations, melt-proofed by a hard candy shell. Red, orange, green, even violet ones. Another time, he sprinkled his letter with his airman words—*gremlins* and *dodos, gubbins* and *penguins*—until it felt like he was right here in the room with us. But she hasn't brought us a letter in a long time. Poor Mrs. Flynn.

Around eleven, it's warm enough for us to take our lunches

outside. The girls settle onto the front steps and the boys sit on the patch of grass nearby. We unwrap our sandwiches and boiled eggs, our apples and snap peas, eating our fill and lifting our faces to the sun for a hint of summer. This is usually the best and fastest twenty minutes of the day, when Ruby and I can talk above a whisper, when the air smells of grass instead of chalk dust, when parallelograms and trapezoids are behind us for the time being.

But not today. Ruby and I barely plunk ourselves down when who marches up the front walk but Irene Kava. Her face is half hidden behind her round sunglasses, but I can still see her crossness. With her lips flat as the pages of a book and her eyebrows tugged down out of sight, she moves like a hurricane. Irene Kava isn't walking—she's storming.

"We had a fire last night," she announces to no one in particular, and to everyone. She holds her white cardigan closed, like she's protecting herself from the next disaster.

Everyone stares at her for a moment. Then Eddie Engen points his apple at her and says, "Your house?"

"Of course, my house," she snips. "Well, the shed next to it. It was *arrrrr*son." She draws out the word like it's a whole paragraph, and then she says it again. "Arson."

Everyone starts to murmur, the boys sitting cross-legged on the grass, the girls sitting press-kneed on the steps, like a buzzing beehive.

"We think it might be the Japs coming home from the camps," Irene says. She's talking about the internment camps President Roosevelt set up after Japan attacked Pearl Harbor. How all the Japanese Americans on the West Coast were forced to move into the camps for fear they'd spy for Japan. How the camps are closing now and the people are being freed.

Irene takes a step back likes she's making room for all the sympathy she expects is coming her way. "That's right. The Japs."

"What are you talking about, Irene?" Eddie asks. "Bly's never had a single Jap."

"But they might be passing through," she says. "Looking for revenge." In case we didn't hear her the first time, she says it again. "Revenge. And anyone could be the next victim. Anyone at all."

"Naw," says Eddie. "They're just glad to be free. They're not gonna do anything that's gonna land them in jail."

Joan Patzke offers a meek "Yeah." Which could mean she agrees with Eddie, but it's probably just because she has a big fat crush on him.

Irene folds her arms tight against her sweater. "Well then, Eddie, are you saying it was someone local?" She takes off her sunglasses so she can aim accusing eyeballs at all of us. "Someone from Bly who did it?"

"Serves her right, the crumb," Ruby says into my ear.

I nod. What else can I do?

"Look at her, planted there like she's waiting for someone to confess," Ruby adds.

"I'm sorry, what was that, Ruby Houlihan?" Irene struts over, shoes clicking.

"Nothing." Ruby sits up a little taller. "I was saying what a crummy thing to have happen."

Irene parks her sunglasses on the top of her head. "You look so sure of yourself. Almost like you know something. Something you aren't telling me."

I finally speak up. "Irene, Ruby doesn't know squat. How could she?"

Irene turns her cutting blue eyes on me. "She could if she had something to do with it." She lowers her voice and leans in. "Or if that grandfather of hers had something to do with it. Didn't I hear he lost his factory job 'cause he couldn't keep up?"

Ruby's mouth falls open but no words come out. Her eyes widen with . . . I can't tell what. I don't know whether she's going to burst into tears or rip Irene's head off.

"Irene!" I shout loud enough for everyone to hear. "Ruby's grandpa serves on the volunteer fire squad. He ran the milkweed collection. He grows his own vegetables. Even if he knows what a wretched thing you are, he has better things to do than light matches in your shed."

I don't think anyone has ever dressed Irene down before. She doesn't know what to do. She opens her mouth, closes it, looks around to see who's watching, unfolds her arms, refolds them, and finally stomps straight past us into the building.

All eyes point to me now, like I am the north and they are compass needles. Some of the eyes smile like little victory signs. Others radiate pity, for I am the girl who has crossed Bly's very own wicked witch. Then they go back to eating their lunches.

"Thanks, Nellie," Ruby says when she finds her voice.

"She deserved it." I wink.

"Yeah, but you didn't have to do it, so thanks. You're a real killer diller."

"You're welcome, Rubes."

Her shoulders loosen a little. "What a chucklehead, huh?"

"The worst."

A hint of a smile appears on Ruby's face.

After lunch, Ruby and I go down to the littlest ones' class-room to read to them. It's good practice for me for when I start teaching. Ruby only comes along because she doesn't like geography. Today, we're both extra glad to be here—or any-where Irene Kava isn't.

The room is empty when we show up. We can see out the window that the tots are watering their Victory Garden in the back, growing their own vegetables so there's more for our soldiers to eat. By the time we've rummaged through the bookshelf and made our choices, they're filing in, all pink faces and high-pitched voices, everyone so happy to see us.

For them, war isn't about killing or dying. It's about pretty gardens and special songs and waving flags. It's about that poster on their classroom wall, the one where Mickey Mouse and Donald Duck are telling them, "Join the Victory March." It's about the Schools at War club and those funny Walt Disney cartoons. Well, whatever it takes to get them to help out, I guess.

Ruby takes her group to one side of the room and I take mine to the other. We sit cross-legged on the floor in a little circle. I've chosen *The Adventures of the Wishing-Chair*, about a chair that sprouts wings and takes you wherever you want to go. We only have time for one chapter, so I read the one where Peter and Mollie go to Mr. Grim's School for Bad Brownies, which isn't nearly as scary as it sounds. When I finish, I ask the little kids where they'd go if they had a magical chair.

"The North Pole," squeaks Tommy Doyle.

"The Tooth Fairy's mountain," says the girl they call Fred but whose name is really Frederique.

On the other side of the room, the children burst out laughing as Ruby acts out her story. For someone who doesn't want to be a teacher, she's pretty good with kids. I guess she really hates geography class.

"Where would you go, Nellie?" asks Danny DuBois. They all stare at me.

"Me? I guess I'd wish to go . . . to the moon. To see if it's really made of cheese."

They think this is hilarious. There might be hope for me as a teacher yet. And the first thing I'll teach my class is all about the night sky.

Suddenly, the end-of-day bell rings even though it's scarcely noon. An air-raid drill. At least, everyone hopes it's only a drill. We can never be sure. Even these smallest of children know that. Fred's eyes rim with tears, and Danny DuBois throws his arms around me.

"Hush," I say over the din of the bell. "Everything's fine. We're just pretending."

Ruby and I help the teacher get the children lined up facing the wall. A few of them forget to cover their heads with their hands, but they all know what to do: stand quietly until the bell stops ringing. No bathroom breaks, no whispering to a neighbor, no pinching the friend next to you. In the older classrooms, everyone is crouching under their desks, straining to hear the whistle of a bomb, wondering if this time it's for real, if anyone will survive, or if all those blankets, candles, and tins of food stacked in the closet will go to waste.

This is the longest three minutes ever. The three minutes when you don't know if a fourth minute will follow. When you hate the murderous enemy more than ever. When you wish your pa were here to make everything okay again. Finally, the bell stops, and the silence sounds like music.

8

TAMIKO

November 3, 1944

I can hardly believe it—my wish has come true! I made Suki
pinch me to make sure I wasn't dreaming. At school today, we
were told that we'll be leaving for the theater! The Emperor's
Imperial Army needs girls with nimble hands to build . . . something, I don't know what. We'll finally be doing something to help
the war, to help Kyo, to help create the universal brotherhood.

All the girls in our class will be going to Kure City, so I'll
have Suki with me. There will be girls from other schools too.
The best news is that they'll feed us. Real meals for three months,
maybe longer. Which leaves more food at home for Auntie.
What else is there to know?

On the walk home from school now, I don't feel my bad hip.
I don't even feel the road beneath my feet. I'm floating.

"What do you think we'll be building?" Suki asks.

I adjust my pile of books and think. "They want agile hands,
so maybe it's something fragile."

"Or small."

"Or intricate."

"But what?" she asks.

"Medals for our war heroes, perhaps. Or warm clothes for the soldiers. Or feasts for the troops in training."

Suki shrugs. "Those are things you make. Eguchi-sensei said *build*."

"It must be something important," I say.

"Well, as long as they feed us well, I don't care if we're digging latrines. I'd do anything for a nice hot bowl of miso soup."

"Or fried tofu."

"With sweet soy sauce dip," she says. "And a crab and cucumber salad on the side."

"No more!" I laugh.

We reach our turning-off point, but we're not done marveling.

"I wonder where we'll sleep at night," I say. "Right at the theater, I suppose."

I smile at that.

"Tamiko?" she says.

"Yes?"

"Let's stick together in Kure. Starting with the bus ride there."

"Like glue," I tell her. "How's that?"

She gives me her brightest smirky grin.

"See you tomorrow," I say, and float the rest of the way home.

When I get to the cottage, there's even more good news. A letter from Kyo! Auntie's eyes twinkle as she hands it to me, so I know it's a cheerful note. At least, it's not a painful note—Kyo is all right. At least, he was all right when he wrote it. I unfold the paper and read.

Dear Auntie and Tamiko,

How are you? I am well. I'm not allowed to tell you where I am, but it doesn't really matter, since we'll probably have moved on by the time you receive this. I'm a fully trained soldier now—my whole group is. We've learned to use weapons, carry out maneuvers, and survive during the most difficult situations.

I'm glad to have the honor of serving the Emperor's way. When I return from this war, I'll bring you victory and joy. Right now, though, I must sleep—mornings come very early here.

Your loyal nephew, brother, and soldier,

~ Kyo

P.S. I received your Daruma doll, Tamiko. I believe it helped me this week. But that's another story.

I read the letter again. *I am well.* It's music. *I'll bring you victory and joy.* It's a beautiful prayer. *Your loyal brother.* It's perfect.

I return the letter to my aunt. I know she'll want to keep it with her always. "Thank you," I say. "And now I have something to tell you."

I sit her down at the low table in the sitting room and tell her everything I know about the Kure adventure. She perches quietly on her cushion as I rave about the theater and nimble fingers and the Emperor's Imperial Army. It tumbles out of me in a single breath, all my excitement, like a sneeze that has been waiting all day to burst free. When I finally come up for air, I look for the pride I'm sure will be gleaming in her eyes.

It isn't there.

"Auntie? Aren't you pleased?"

She lowers her chin. "No, my dear, I'm not."

"Why?"

"It doesn't matter why. You have no choice but to leave. I have no choice but to let you go."

"But Auntie, when I'm in Kure, we'll both have more to eat. In a few days, we'll both be better off."

"When you speak of tomorrow, the rats in the ceiling laugh."

"Let them laugh," I say, louder than I mean to. "The rats are wrong this time."

Auntie folds her hands into a ball. "You don't know when you'll leave for Kure. Or what you'll be doing there. Or how long you'll stay. Yet you're certain."

"And you're troubled."

She doesn't answer.

"I'll miss you, Auntie."

"Don't miss me, Tamiko. Come back to me."

"I'll come home so plump, you might not even recognize me."

"Then it's lucky you have a birthmark on your shoulder."

She pushes herself slowly up to standing, looking a little older than when she sat down.

Kyo,

Thank you for your letter. I couldn't wait to get home from school today to write you with my news. Like you, I'll soon be serving our Emperor's Imperial Army. I'll be one of the hundred million hearts beating as one.

My classmates and I will leave shortly for Kure to begin building. We don't know what we'll be making exactly, but surely it will be useful to the army. It's the right thing to do. Besides, I'll have Suki with me, and there will be food in abundance. Our aunt doesn't share my gladness yet. She'll come around, though, when she has twice as much rice to herself.

We'll be allowed to bring only a change of clothes and a few washing necessaries to Kure. Everything else, including my paper and pen, will stay at home, so this will be my last letter to you for a while. But I'll pray for you every day, and Auntie will pray for both of us. We only wish we knew where you are, now that you've finished training. Be safe, Kyo.

~ Tamiko

We're all called to the gymnasium this afternoon—our last day of school. When we get there, we find an officer from the air base. He tells us an army bus will pick us up in the morning. That we will help bring peace to the nation, to the world. He tells us to wear comfortable clothes and to pack lightly. Then he tells us what we'll be building in Kure City.

Balloons! Ten thousand paper balloons, each one as wide as a house, floating high on icy currents. We're not told why. For our soldiers to fly on patrol? To make food drops to the people? I smile to think that one day I may look up and see Kyo smiling down in an airship I have made. *A Daruma doll and a shrine offering are good,* he'll call down to me. *But a balloon is better.*

Lying on my futon tonight, I don't care that I'm going to bed hungry. All night I'll dream of flying things, of kites and cranes, of dandelions on the wind, of shooting stars and dragonfly wings. Soon I'll be fed. Soon I'll serve our Emperor by making his balloons.

Through my closed eyes, I see my father. I remember I used to beg him to take me to the paper balloon festival in Kamihinokinai. I wanted to watch the enormous balloons rise into the wintry night sky. I wanted to see how they were painted with fierce samurai and beautiful women and words of hope. I wanted to make a wish on them so they could carry my dream to the heavens. I didn't understand when he told me the city was a thousand kilometers away. All I wanted was to be near the paper balloons. And now I will be. Suki and I and the other girls.

Funny, I wonder what I would have wished for then, back when I already had everything and everyone I needed.

9

NELLIE

May 1, 1945

After the real end-of-day bell rings, the twins and I drop Ruby off at her house. I'm glad it's Friday. Even though I have a pile of homework, and even though I have to get up early tomorrow for the salvage drive, it's still the weekend. Two days—two and a half days if you count the rest of today—without math or geography or Irene Kava. It's not that I don't like school. I just like the weekends better.

We stand at Ruby's front walk for a bit. She jabbers away about something or other, but I'm busy looking over at Joey's house, hoping I might spot him coming back from his day of farm work.

"Am I interrupting?" Ruby says.

"Hmm?"

"Have you been listening to a single word?"

"Well, I—"

"Can we go into the cage now?" Willie interrupts. "Please, Ruby?"

She makes a fake frown at him.

"Puh-lease?" he pleads.

"It's an aviary, Willie, not a cage," she says.

"Well, can we?"

"I suppose. Don't forget to close the door behind you." The twins race off to see the doves, and Ruby turns back to me. "I said, what time are you gonna pick me up tomorrow?"

"Well, we have to be at the drive by nine. So eight thirty, I guess. How's that?"

"Fine. You wearing trousers?"

My gaze slips back to the Coopers' house.

"Nellie?"

"Oh, sorry. What was that?"

"What's gotten into you today, Nellie Bly? This morning, you were about to fall asleep on your feet. Now you can't pay attention to a word I say. What's going on?"

I rejuggle my books. "I . . . nothing. Still tired, that's all."

"Then go to bed early tonight or something. Now, are you going to wear trousers or not?"

"I will if you will."

"Deal."

"I did not!" Henry's voice rises above our chatter.

"Did too," counters Willie.

I roll my eyes. "Are the birds all right?"

"Yes," they both call.

"Come on then, time to get home."

For a change, they both mind me. In a moment, they run in our direction.

"Did you close the door?" Ruby asks.

"Yup," pants Willie.

"Did you lock it?" she asks.

The boys stop short. "Did you lock it?" Willie asks Henry.

"Nope," says Henry. "Did you?"

Ruby points a finger toward the side of the house. The boys dash back to the aviary, then go tearing across the yard toward home.

"Hey!" I scold. "Don't you have something to say to Ruby?"

They halt and look at each other, mystified. "See you on Monday?" Henry ventures.

"Try again."

"Thank you? Yeah, thank you for letting us into the cage."

"The aviary," I correct him.

"Yeah, that's what I meant."

"See you in the morning, Rubes," I say. "Eight thirty."

The boys run ahead while I stroll up the road. When I reach our mailbox, I spot Joey sitting on his front steps, looking at a comic book, probably Captain America—that's his favorite.

I wish I could go over and sit down next to him, peek over his shoulder. I'd tell him about Irene Kava, how she came to school late and blamed the fire on the Japanese folks. I might even tell him I know the truth, that his secret is safe with me, that he's still my best friend.

"Hey, Joey," I call across the street, trying to sound casual.

He looks up, and I see his nose got burned from the day out in the sun. "Hey, Nellie," he answers. No smile, no wave.

"You missed an air-raid drill today."

He nods.

I pull open the mailbox door. "See you at the drive tomorrow?"

"Yup." And then he goes back to his comics.

I want to ask him about the cows, but then I notice the envelope stuck in the back of our mailbox. A letter from Pa! I rip it open right there on the street—it's addressed to the whole family, so it's as much mine as it is Mother's. In Pa's scratchy handwriting, he says:

Hello all,

I hope this note finds you well. Dotty darling, I hate that I wasn't there for your birthday last week, but I'll make up for it in spades when I return, which can't be soon enough.

Boys, since I know how much you like birds, I will tell you that our cook has befriended a puffin. The funny little fellow, with its bright orange beak and legs, seems quite fond of mess hall fare. You should look these birds up in your school encyclopedia when you can.

Nellie, the temperature warmed up to 30 degrees yesterday, and the clouds lifted too, so it was a perfect night for skygazing. And what did I see but the northern lights in all their otherworldly green glory. One day, when this war is over and the world is at peace, perhaps we will come north to see this marvel together.

I love you all. Take care of each other.

~ Bill / Pa

I push the letter back into the envelope and hold it to my chest, feeling Pa next to my heart. I relish this moment, when Pa's words belong to me, when I don't have to share them with Mother or the twins. Just for these few seconds, Pa is mine. He'll be all mine again when we travel to the northern lights together someday. I can hardly wait.

Then I glance back across the street. Poor Joey. While I have Pa's return to look forward to, and his letters to read in the meantime, Joey doesn't have anything from his brother, not a thing. No wonder he doesn't feel like talking. I close the mailbox and head inside.

Mother's face is a stewed tomato from scrubbing the kitchen. Her friend Mrs. Wells is going to drop by, so she wants everything to look fresh. She has sent Henry and Willie upstairs to change their clothes, with strict orders to play outside till her company leaves. Then she hands me a bowl of peas to shell out on the back stoop.

"Oh!" she breathes when she sees the envelope in my hand.

I trade the envelope for the bowl of peas. "From Pa," I tell her, but she's already reading the letter. There's a smile on her face, the smile she hardly ever brings out anymore, the smile she used to wear all the time before Pa went to war.

I watch her eyes go back and forth across the lines. She reaches the bottom and starts again at the top. Then she puts the letter in her apron pocket and loses her smile. "Go on now, I have to finish up here before Mrs. Wells arrives."

With the windows wide open, I can hear everything Mother and Mrs. Wells say. The best part is when Mrs. Wells sets her coffee cup down with a clink and declares, "Dotty, remember how we were going to run off to Hollywood as soon as we finished school?"

"We were going to be starlets, all champagne and pearls by the time we were old enough to vote," Mother says.

It's hard to think of Mother being starry-eyed like that once upon a time. It's hard even to think of her being young. I mean, I know she was young once, but I can't picture her acting young. Having dreams, ambition, wanderlust. That kind of stuff. And Mrs. Wells, well, her family runs the cardboard box factory over near Hildebrand. It doesn't get much more boring than that.

"Incoming!" Willie scampers into the backyard, Henry right behind him. "Take cover! Every man for himself!" They run under the old kiddie slide and crouch down, covering their heads.

Mother comes over to the window. "For heaven's sake, boys, what's going on?"

"We're practicing our air-raid drills," Henry calls back.

"Well, please do it more quietly." She closes the window with a snap. My eavesdropping is over, thanks to the bothersome ones.

"Wanna play with us?" Henry asks me.

"Nope. Wanna shell peas?"

"Nope."

"Can I have some?" Willie comes out from under the slide.

"Not till supper."

"But I'm hungry. I gave half my sandwich to Jimmy Hall. He forgot his lunch again."

Jimmy Hall probably didn't forget his lunch today or any

other day. He probably doesn't have a lunch to bring some days, what with rationing and his six brothers and sisters. Maybe I should start sending an extra sandwich when I can.

"Fine," I say, "but you have to do the shelling yourself." I give them each a handful of pods. They run off, shouting about a grenade in the front yard. I hope Joey's mother doesn't hear their game.

After a while, Mrs. Wells goes home, and we make scrambled eggs and peas for supper. Later on, the sun goes behind the hills, the blackout curtains go down, and I go out back. It's cool tonight, so I sit on the Adirondack chair with a blanket spread on my lap and the kiddie slide next to me. Tree frogs keep me company, and somewhere an owl hoots. I use my spyglass to spot Saturn—oh, and there's Jupiter, her red spot like an eye gazing down at me. The Seven Sisters, the Herdsman, they're all here tonight.

No falling stars, though, no fairy lights or magic. Too bad I forgot to wish on the one I saw last night.

Pa told me how the ancients came up with the wishing idea. They thought the gods sometimes peeled away the veil between heaven and earth to look at people. When they did, a few stars would slip out and become shooting stars. So when people saw a shooting star, they knew the gods were looking down at them, and figured it was the perfect time to ask for something.

Not that I really believe in that sort of thing, but what's the harm? There are lots of things to wish for. For Japan and Germany to fall so Pa can come. For Joey to be my best friend again. For Mother to give me the time of day. Well, at least I have the night sky with me. I always have that.

When a coyote starts crying, lonesome for the moon, I give him his privacy and head inside.

10

TAMIKO

November 10, 1944

Otoosan and Okaasan,

Today we go to Kure City and I'll make my first balloon! I don't have any idea how to make one, of course. None of us does. Perhaps I'll be called on to stitch a rising sun on them, each one a brilliant red. Ten thousand suns to light our nights and brighten our days. Ten thousand suns to honor our sun goddess, Amaterasu. I woke up happy just thinking about it this morning.

Auntie isn't pleased, though. Not even close. She's not worried the way she was when Kyo left—I won't be fighting enemy soldiers, after all. But she's even more sad, for now she'll be all alone. Try as she might to hide it, the gloom darkens her eyes. I want to leave something of myself behind for her, but what? What can I leave that will warm her heart during this long, solitary winter?

~ Tamiko

As I'm about to put my diary away, I have an idea. I tear out a sheet of paper and leave this haiku for Auntie in the kitchen:

December winds knock
On your door with my message
I'll be home by spring.

Quickly, I pack my few things, change into trousers, and eat a small bowl of gray rice. Then I'm off to school, where the army bus will pick us up and take us to Kure City.

The bus hasn't arrived yet when I get to the schoolyard. Some of the other girls stand out front, their rucksacks thrown into a pile. I add mine to the heap and join them. It's cold out, so we huddle together. Suki arrives, and one by one so do the rest of the girls in our class. The pile is now a hill, and the sun is climbing, but still no bus.

Two or three of the girls are teary-eyed, as if they don't want to go, as if they'd rather be stuck at home than help the army and get real meals. I hear one girl named Keiko say, "I cut off a lock of my hair and pressed it into one of my mother's books. In case I don't come home." I don't understand these girls.

"What time is it?" someone asks.

"Almost nine," another girl answers.

Suki rubs her arms for warmth. "I thought they were supposed to be here at eight."

"They were," I say.

We stand around a while longer, jumping in place for heat, talking in excited tones, watching our breath turn to fog. Then

Suki spies a soldier walking across the schoolyard. I think he's the same one who came last week to tell us about the balloons. Yes, I recognize his mustache. The soldier walks past us but doesn't say hello or even nod. He goes straight inside the school, leaving us to wonder where the bus is parked.

Five minutes later, our teacher, Eguchi-sensei, comes out of the school. He looks tired, his head down. Or maybe he's worried about something. He stops next to a girl named Chiyo. Chiyo is the smallest girl in our class, and she walks with a crutch—she had polio too, worse than mine. Eguchi-sensei says something into Chiyo's ear, something that makes her frown. I feel sorry for her.

Then Eguchi-sensei walks over to me. "May I see you in the classroom?"

Now I feel sorry for me. When the two lame girls get called out together, it's never good. It's always the first step in treating us differently, treating us unfairly.

"I'll be right back," I tell Suki.

"All right." She feels sorry for me too—I can see it in her eyes. She probably also feels glad—glad she's not the one getting singled out. Glad she doesn't have a limp, or a brother off to war, or an aunt who's all by herself now.

I expect to see the soldier in the classroom, but he's not there. It's just Sensei, Chiyo, and me.

"Girls," our teacher tells us. "There will be no bus today. Everyone who goes to Kure City will have to walk."

"I can do that," I blurt.

Sensei nods and grips his hands behind his back. "I believe

you could. But our soldier has instructions. Anyone who is lame must be sent home."

I glance at Chiyo. I see relief on her face. She wants to stay home. She has probably never been away, not even last summer when we were all sent out to work the rice paddies. This is good news for her. But not for me. I want to help. I can help.

"Eguchi-sensei," I try again. "The soldier won't even have to know I'm lame. I can hide my limp. Watch."

It's not easy, but I walk to the door and back with hardly a hobble. All I have to do is go down harder on my good leg. Then it looks almost even. "You see?"

"I see," Sensei says. "I see that you're eager. But it won't do. I've already discussed it with the soldier."

"But I can slip right in. He'll never notice, I promise."

"He will notice. He knows there are twenty-seven girls out there right now, not twenty-eight. Twenty-seven. It's done."

"But I want to help." My throat aches with the tears I hold back. "I must help."

"You can help," he says. "You can help your family at home. And you can study. We'll have no school while the others are in Kure City. Bring your books home and teach yourself something."

"But—"

"It's done. Go home, girls. And take heart. You may be glad you didn't go."

"How could I be glad?" I groan to myself, but also loud enough for him to hear.

"It may not be everything you imagine there." Unease flashes across his face again. "It may not be anything at all like you imagine."

"Yes, Sensei," I mumble, but the words are glass shards in my mouth.

"Goodbye, girls," he says.

"Thank you, Sensei," we say. I think Chiyo hides a little smile as we leave the classroom.

I stop in the bathroom on the way out. I need to buy some time, think of a plan, give Chiyo a chance to leave. Because I'm not going to surrender. I'm not going to give up my one chance to do the right thing. If I can just find a way to get around the soldier and his instructions about twenty-seven girls. There has to be a way.

All the girls are still standing around the schoolyard, except for a couple who are sitting on their rucksacks. Suki spies me walking toward the flock and waves. I raise a finger to my lips so she won't call to me. Anyone could be listening, watching—the soldier, Eguchi-sensei, Chiyo, anyone. I must be quiet as a forest, swift as the wind, insistent as a mosquito.

I slip next to Keiko, one of the girls who was crying earlier. She lives alone with her mother while her father serves in the war. Keiko makes beautiful calligraphy in art class. Once she spent an hour writing out a poem I penned for Auntie's birthday. Now I can do something for her.

"Hello, Keiko," I say.

She looks up from whatever daydream she's in. "Hello, Tamiko."

"I want to tell you something. A secret."

She doesn't look interested. Her mind is on other things. On Kure. On leaving home.

"Listen," I whisper. "The soldier told Eguchi-sensei that only twenty-seven girls may go to Kure. Our class has twenty-nine."

A faint light glints in her eyes.

"Sensei offered Chiyo and me to stay back, because of our legs. Chiyo already went home. But I still want to go."

Her lips part. She's daring to hope.

"Do you want to switch places with me?" I ask.

Keiko glances over her shoulder at the other girls. Then she turns back to me and nods. "How?" she asks.

"All you have to do is steal away. The soldier only knows our number, not our names or faces."

Her eyes well up again, this time with relief.

"Do it now," I whisper. "Before the soldier comes back. In case Sensei comes out. Grab your rucksack and go."

She doesn't even say goodbye. She rushes to the pile, finds her rucksack, and run-walks down the road. In a minute, she's out of sight.

From the other side of the group, Suki cocks her head at me. She wants to know what this is all about. I'll tell her, but she won't understand. How could she? She's never had to fight for her rightful place. She's never had to break the rules just to be included.

I give Suki a short shake of my head. She'll have to wait. I'll tell her everything—later.

We walk for two hours, the soldier and us girls, in silence the whole way. This is longer than I've ever hiked in my life.

Suki and I stay to the back of the line, away from the soldier's stare, just in case. The first hour isn't so bad. I feel the fire-horse, but I force my mind away from the beast. I focus instead on balloons, on food, on serving our Emperor. As we get closer to the city on the Inland Sea, I think I smell salt, the symbol of purity, and it makes me glad. For the first time, I know how Kyo felt marching off to war.

The second hour is grueling. Another fire-horse joins the old familiar one. Then another and another appear, charging across my hip and around to my back. I'm having trouble keeping up. Suki loops her arm through mine, and I lean on her without meaning to, without wanting to. It's still cold out, and now I'm hungry as well. But I can't stop, can't even slow down. I must be like the carp fish.

That's another one of Grandmother's stories. One long ago winter, a painter stood by a pond, making a picture of the iced-over water and the snowy banks. As he worked, he kept hearing a tap-tap-tapping noise coming from the pond. He stepped closer and saw a carp trying to reach a rice biscuit that lay on top of the ice. The fish was ramming its head against the ice, hoping to break through to the food. Amazed, the painter watched the carp spend three full hours attacking the ice. First the ice cracked, then a little hole opened, then a larger hole. Finally, the ice collapsed, and the exhausted, bruised carp got its reward.

The carp persisted. And so will I. No more frightened girl like I was at the village shrine, when I could barely lift a tin coin. I'll show Suki how strong I am. I'll prove to the kami how worthy I am. I'll honor my duty to my brother and my country.

"We're here!" I squeeze Suki's elbow when we finally, finally cross into Kure City.

She puts out her palm to catch the first raindrops. "Just in time, too."

The soldier tells us all to walk faster—we still have a way to go. I rub my howling hip and try to keep up.

"Are you all right?" Suki asks.

"Fine." I train my attention on the shipyards and the sea beyond. I wonder if Kyo went to war on a vessel docked here. The rain falls in cold, sharp snaps. To cheer me up, Suki starts singing a rainy-day nursery rhyme. "Uh-oh, that girl is dripping wet," she purrs as softly as she can. "That girl is crying under the willow. Pitch pitch goes the rain. Chap chap. Run run!"

"Suki, hush," I scold. "You're going to get us in trouble."

She smirks and we trudge on, down the one road that sprouts into many streets, until we're in the heart of the city. The soldier takes us into a small office building, where the halls are stacked with cotton mats for us to sleep on. I'd do anything to collapse onto one of them right now, to rest my leg and ward off the fire-horses, but there's no time for that.

We drop off our few things—a blanket, a change of clothes. Then we go upstairs to a room where a man in uniform—a boy, really—stands behind a table piled with strange-looking gadgets. On the wall over his head is a whole row of that famous poster, the one with the skull saying, "Hello, Americans! I'll be your guide now."

We all cram into the room and wait for the soldier to show us what we need to know. Very exciting! Suki and I clutch hands.

The soldier isn't tall, but he seems to tower over us, standing so straight and alert in his uniform. A prick of electricity pulses through my belly, partly because I'm eager for him to teach us about the paper, and partly because he's terribly handsome, with his square face and noble air. I glance at Suki, who bites her lip. I can tell she's trying her best not to smile her smirkish smile. She's trying very hard.

The first thing the soldier does is to look us solemnly in the eye. He doesn't say good morning or ask us how our trek here was. He doesn't tell us his name. He simply holds up a piece of paper the size of a tatami mat, a beautiful sheet of paper, the kind you'd use for origami or calligraphy or lanterns or kites, all white and translucent. His fingers are slender, assured.

"This is your new tool," he says, his voice deeper than I expected. "This is how you will vanquish the Americans. This is how we will unite the world under one roof."

We whisper eagerly to each other, but the soldier has no patience for such silliness. He sets the sheet down.

"Much labor has already been done to make this paper," he tells us. "Mulberry branches have been grown, cut, soaked, boiled, stripped of their bark. Boiled again, run under ice-cold streams, bleached. Laid on a rock and beaten to a pulp for hours. Stretched and soaked again."

If he's trying to scare us, it works. So much energy has already been put into the paper! We must not let those efforts go to waste. We have to learn fast, work quickly, attend to every detail. Our nation is counting on us. This handsome soldier is counting on us. Kyo and Auntie and the mulberry farmers are counting on us. It's our duty and our privilege.

"Comrades have toiled over vats of liquid paper," the soldier goes on. "Dipping their screens into the mixture. Shaking, spreading, drying. All so you will have the finest paper to work with."

No one makes a sound. The soldier steps over to a wooden rack on the table. "Watch carefully. This is what you're here for. This is how you will serve our Emperor."

He dips a brush into a small tub of bluish glue and spreads it onto the rack. "This glue is made of konnyaku potatoes," he says. "Don't squander it."

He places two sheets of paper side by side on top of the glue and brushes out any air bubbles. "Now you must let the paper dry," he says. "But not too dry, or it will crack and be unusable."

Someone in the back coughs. The soldier flashes her a glare.

"You'll apply another layer of glue and paper, then another," he goes on. "Five layers. You'll each have two racks, so you can be working at all times."

More excited whispers.

The soldier looks at us grimly. "Each balloon requires six hundred sheets. That means six million sheets of washi paper for Emperor Hirohito. Girls throughout the nation must work their utmost!"

That makes us quiet right down.

"Now it's time to learn with your hands," he says. And we do. The soldier has each one of us practice brushing the potato glue and the paper. The job isn't difficult, but it's nerve-racking with him standing over us, with all the other girls watching, with the Emperor's divine plan at stake.

When it's Suki's turn, I hear the tremble in her breath. She grips me like a tourniquet, like she doesn't want to leave my side. I feel sorry for her . . . even though it feels good to think that maybe, just maybe, she needs me as much as I need her. Well, almost as much.

"You'll be fine," I whisper, extracting my fingers from hers. "I'm right here."

She walks to the front, avoiding the soldier's gaze and picking up the brush with a tight fist. The brush looks awkward in her hand, like a half-strangled snake, but she manages to get a scoopful of the glue onto it. When she brushes the air out of the paper, her movements are much heavier than the soldier's, but they get the job done. She sets down the brush triumphantly.

Now it's my turn, and the prick in my belly turns into a stab. Suki leans in to my ear and says, "It's not bad, you'll see."

"All right."

"And stop holding your breath."

I let out the lungful of air I didn't know I was holding in.

Then I walk to the front, making very sure not to limp.

At the table, I run a finger across the stack of paper. It's gloriously soft and warm, light but also strong. Yes, I can do this. I must do this. I glue my two sheets and look to the soldier for his approval. He doesn't meet my eyes.

After our lesson, we go back downstairs, where we're given dried sardines, white rice, pickled radishes, and potato chips for supper. "Such a feast!" I say to Suki, joining her on her mat. Gingerly, she taps her chopsticks to her bowl, as if she can't believe it's real. "White rice. This is better than a bowl full of pearls."

I take a mouthful of fish. "Mmm."

"If they feed us girls this well, imagine what Kyo is getting," Suki says.

"Hopefully, all the white rice he can gobble."

We eat the rest of our food in silence, quickly, eagerly. Now that real food is finally in front of me, my hunger explodes like a struck hornets' nest. I'm suddenly so ravenous, I do something dishonorable—to Suki, of all people. It happens when a few girls at the other end of the hall start singing a marching song. Suki looks over her shoulder to watch them, and while her head is turned, I take one of her radish slices. Radishes are my brother's favorite.

It's in my mouth before I can stop myself. So delicious, it tastes even better than the radishes in my own bowl. It tastes like I'm getting a little bit extra to make up for all the things I must do without. It tastes like victory.

I chew and swallow the morsel so fast, I have no time to regret it. It was just one little radish, anyway. Just this once. We're all going to be fed like this every day now, so what's the harm?

When someone comes to call an early lights-out, we all find our mats and our blankets. As I lie in the darkness, looking up at the ceiling, imagining it's the endless sky, I smile. I can hardly remember the last time I went to bed with a full belly. I'm immensely grateful to be here, especially since I almost got sent home at the last minute. I know I'll sleep well tonight, even though there's no heat in the building.

11
NELLIE
May 2, 1945

Ruby and I show up at school bright and early for the salvage drive. The yard is already buzzing with people setting up the collection stations—steel in front of the flag, tin next to the chokecherry tree, rubber over by the fence. Eddie Engen is directing traffic in the small parking lot. Joan Patzke and her brother, Dick, are setting up boxes at the rubber station. A few teachers are helping out wherever they can.

Ruby is on refreshment duty, so she heads inside while I try to figure out where I can be useful out here. I scan the yard and quickly decide on the tin station.

"Morning," I say to Joey, who's setting out cardboard boxes behind the small TIN sign on the table. He's wearing a fresh white shirt and old blue jeans with a small rip in one knee.

He looks up. "Oh, hey. You on my team?"

"Uh-huh."

Your secret is safe with me. As long as Mr. Kava keeps his mouth closed, your parents never have to find out about the shed. No one has to find out, not the police, not school, not anyone.

"How about you make a bigger sign?" he says. "Paper and crayons on the table." He reaches into his shirt pocket. "Here's a pen."

When I take the pen, I can smell Aqua Velva on him, which is funny because he doesn't need to shave yet. Maybe he's trying to turn himself into his older brother. Maybe he's trying to act like he's grown up. But starting a fire isn't grown up, if you ask me. What happened to the Joey who used to play ball and listen to the wireless and stop by the house every weekend?

"Make it big enough to see from the road," he adds.

I fill up the poster paper with the word TIN, each letter outlined in black and a different color on the inside—red, white, and blue. I do it like it's the most important thing in the world, and in a way, it is. It's the best thing us Bly kids can do for the war effort. And it's the thing us Bly kids *should* be doing for the war effort, not stuffing ourselves with potatoes and sneaking on to the front lines. I sure hope Joey isn't getting any stupid ideas about picking up where Peter left off.

Old Mr. Swanson, who used to run the filling station, is our first customer. He looks sheepish as he comes forward with two bags of loot. "Now you know how many biscuits I ate since the last drive," he confesses. "Eight tins, and I emptied them all by myself."

"That's not so bad." I take the tins from him. "Our last drive was clear back in September, after all."

Joey takes the tins from me so I can help the next customer.

As he does, our hands brush, almost like our fingers are kissing. Does he even notice? Probably not.

Behind me, someone says, "Hello there, Joey." I turn to see Irene Kava putting on her flirtiest voice. She's dressed like she's going to a party, with a navy blue checked dress and a red tam hat, and is holding out a box of tins like it's a gift for the host— the host being Joey.

Well, of course this is a party to her. Her father didn't have to go to war. He'll never have to go to war. He'll stay right here running the logging mill and buying her new dresses and hats. I hate her.

Joey looks up from the tin pile. "Hey, Irene." He takes a step in her direction, but I'm faster than he is.

"I'll get this." I put my hands on her box. "Thanks, Irene."

She scowls, but there's nothing she can do. I walk the box over to Joey, who carries it to the pile and starts sorting it. I hope she hates me for it. I hope she hates me twice as much as I hate her.

"My," Irene says to Joey's back, "you sure are getting a lot of business, from the looks of it."

"Uh-huh," Joey says absently.

"Hope this little bit I brought helps."

"Hmm, yup."

"Thanks again for stopping by, Irene." I flash her my widest grin. "See you on Monday."

I can almost see the smoke building up between her ears.

"Joey," she says with more sugar than a frosted donut. "Did you know your little helper here used a very unladylike word on me yesterday?"

Joey turns around.

Irene steps toward him. "Nellie Doud had the nerve to call me a wretch."

His gaze shifts to me. "You did?"

I nod. I'm not ashamed of it. Irene *is* a wretch. A spoiled rotten wretch.

Irene smirks at me, her rosebud lips curled into a sneer. "What do you think of that, Joey?" she coos.

"I think she must've had a good reason," he says and turns right back around to the tin pile.

Take that, I tell Irene with my eyes. *Joey can see right through you.*

Irene's mouth unclasps, but she doesn't say a word, just huffs off, her red tam bobbing like an apple.

Victory!

"What happened between you two, anyway?" Joey asks. He's back to sorting tin.

"Lunchtime yesterday," I say, real casual, hoping Irene can see us talking. "She started spouting off about a fire in her shed."

Joey snaps his head up. Now he's really listening. "A fire?"

"Uh-huh. She was saying how she thinks someone did it for revenge."

His face turns white.

I feel bad for sending him into sweats like this, so I decide to let him off the hook. "Yeah, like maybe the Japanese on their way home from the camps did it."

He lets out a breath.

"Then she accused Ruby's grandpa—can you believe? So I put her in her place, that's all."

"Sounds like she had it coming."

Now that we're actually talking, I don't want it to stop. I blurt out the first thing that comes to my mind. "How come you don't like Irene?"

"I never said I don't like her."

"Oh."

"Even though I don't." Then he stops sorting and looks at me. "Thing is, you see. The thing is—"

"Good morning," comes a voice from behind.

I look up to see Pastor Mitchell and his wife. Well, I guess that's the end of our chin-wag over Irene. *Rats! I want to know what Joey was going to say. Was he about to tell me how mad he is at Mr. Kava, or what he has against Irene?* I want to hear it, hear all about it, but the moment is gone.

12

TAMIKO

November 11, 1944

Today, our first day of work on the secret balloon project, I feel like I'm in the army right alongside Kyo. They wake us up at four thirty in the morning to the tune of "Senyu"—Comrade in Arms. We each get a rice ball for breakfast. It's cold in the hallway, so we move along fast. Then we walk to work, singing the flag march and the song of the fierce eagles. I'm glad it's still dark out so I don't have to hide my limp. Half an hour later, we enter the Fantaji Theater.

The last time I was here, it was to watch a musical revue. The theater seemed to sing then, to glow with spirit and celebration. Now it's transformed into a production factory.

The shell is still here, of course, along with the high ceiling, the wooden stage, the runways, the balcony boxes. But everything else is gone—the seats, the brocade stage curtains, the sets, the aliveness. Now every inch of space is covered with tables full of washi racks. Around the tables, dozens of girls work away with the paper and the glue. They look a little older than us, these girls, and they seem very serious. They're all barefoot.

After a moment, the girls notice we're here. Quickly, they clean up their areas, find their shoes, and file out of the auditorium. Some of them nod to us, some of them bend their heads together in hushed talk. They seem to know what to do and where to go without being told.

"Where do they sleep?" Suki asks. "Why didn't we see them yesterday?"

"I don't know," I say. "Maybe they stay in different offices. Or maybe we take turns sleeping in the same place."

"You think they work all night?"

"I think this place works around the clock," I answer.

Suki opens her mouth to say something, but then the door behind us opens and dozens of other girls stream in. Girls we don't recognize, girls from other schools. Suki and I have to move closer to the stage to make room for the onslaught.

"Everyone!" The handsome soldier from yesterday appears on the stage, calling for our attention.

We all go silent.

"We must get right to work," he says. "Six of you to a table. Remember what you learned yesterday. Work quickly, work carefully. That is all. Begin!"

Suki and I link arms so we won't get separated. We position ourselves at the nearest table, up against the stage. Four girls we don't know join us. We nod to each other but don't speak. We're too excited and nervous to talk.

It doesn't take long to figure out why the other girls went barefoot. The floor is thick with the bluish potato glue that drips off the racks, and our soles get stuck in it. Soon, we all kick off our shoes. There, that's better. We can move faster now.

We labor for twelve straight hours. It's a lot of work—not complicated, just a lot of work—and we're happy to do it. Besides, it's heated in the theater—to help the paper dry—and we had breakfast this morning and supper the night before. We are strong. Before the day is over, Suki and I have learned the names of the other girls at our table. Rin is the small girl next to me. The others are Yoko, Ai, and Yui. They're all from Kure City.

The handsome soldier tells us when our shift is finished. We've been so focused, we haven't even noticed the girls waiting in the back to start their shift. After tidying up our spaces and retrieving our shoes, we file out of the auditorium, just as the older girls did when we arrived this morning.

It's a cold march back to the dorm tonight. We're exhausted but also energized. We've done something useful for our divine nation! And there's still supper to look forward to. Supper ends up being smaller than last night's, though. We each get a bowl of rice mixed with sweet potatoes that are starting to turn black, and a cup of some sort of broth. But the food is hot, and we're cold, and we'll be asleep soon anyway.

I wonder what the handsome soldier is having for his dinner, and where he'll sleep tonight. I wonder too where Kyo is. Is his belly full? Is his canteen filled with fresh water? Is my Daruma doll watching over him yet?

"Tamiko?" Suki says from her mat shortly after lights-out. Even though she's whispering, her voice seems to echo off the low ceiling and bare walls of the narrow hallway.

"Right here," I whisper back—too loud, I guess, because somewhere another girl rolls over with an annoyed sigh. "Are you still hungry?"

I hate to admit that I am. "Why?"

"Wanted to make sure it's not only me."

"It isn't."

"Okay . . . Tamiko?"

"Hmm." I'm getting drowsy. So drowsy I can almost imagine I'm at home on my soft futon. Almost, but not quite. The hard floor pushes up through my thin mat, reminding me where I am.

"Do you believe in unlucky years?" she asks.

"Hmm . . . what?"

"Unlucky ages. You know: nineteen, thirty-three, thirty-seven?"

I roll on my side to face her. "Suki, your first unlucky age is years away. Why are you worrying about it now?"

"Fuyumi. She turns unlucky tomorrow. I forgot to wish her good luck before we left."

I don't say anything right away. First, I have to count to ten. Suki's sister—no, Suki's whole family, they're the luckiest people I know. They're all alive. No one is at war. They've slept together in the same cottage every single night up until now. How dare Suki worry about her sister's fortune?

That's what I think, but it's not what I say. "Don't worry, Suki. Your sister has luck to spare."

"I guess she did get lucky in the looks department. In the getting-attention department." Suki turns onto her back. "I kind of hate her for that. But I still worry for her, for nineteen."

"What year was she born?" I ask. "Tora—the tiger."

"So she's courageous. She can handle anything." A smile creeps onto my lips. "Like the time we put that toad in her futon."

Suki lets out a giggle. "We were mad at her for . . . for . . ."

"For tattling on us when we snooped in her things." I remind her. "We thought we'd get even by scaring her, remember? But she didn't bat an eye when she found the toad. Just scooped it up and dropped it outside. Like I said, she can handle anything."

Suki pulls her arms inside her covers. "You really think so?"

"I know so. We'll all be fine. We're going to win this war."

She lowers herself back down onto her mat. "What year is Kyo?"

"Ushi—ox."

"Good," she says. "Patient, alert. He won't do anything stupid."

"Like volunteering to go to war?"

"That's not stupid," she breathes.

Easy for her to say. I decide to ignore it.

"Hey," she says. "Remember when we had that poster-making contest in art class? And Keiko drew a bunch of Western soldiers surrendering . . . with the slogan 'Every age is unlucky for these guys'?"

I laugh softly at the memory. "Suki?"

"Yes?"

"Are you cold?"

"A little." She tucks her thin blanket a little tighter around her. "Are you?"

"Kind of."

"Here, let's try this." She pushes her mat right next to mine. We combine our blankets and curl up together. It's still cold, but we're together.

Suddenly, I feel terrible for stealing her radish last night. She's as hungry as I am. She's sharing her blanket with me now. She's my best friend. I make a silent promise to be a better friend in return.

Soon Suki's breathing slows into a regular hum. We've all worked hard today. We'll work hard again in the morning. It's time to rest. I pull my feet under the blankets and let the rustlings and snores in the hallway lull me to sleep. At least it will be warm in the theater tomorrow.

13

NELLIE

May 2, 1945

"Morning," I say to Pastor Mitchell and his wife. Joey puts down the box of tin he's sorting and comes over.

I always feel funny when I run into the pastor these days because we haven't been to church since Pa went into the army. Some people go to church because they have someone in the service, people like Mrs. Flynn. But Mother doesn't seem that interested anymore, and besides, the twins can't sit still for more than twenty minutes at a shot. I think Joey stopped going when Peter died.

"How's business today?" Mrs. Mitchell offers her trademark smile and adjusts the brunette bun atop her head.

"Pretty fine," I say. My eyes catch on her front side. I heard she was expecting a baby, but this is the first time it shows on her.

"Got some tin for us?" Joey asks.

"We only had rubber this time," says the pastor, the sun glinting off his round wire glasses. "Say, it's been so warm, we're taking some young people up to Gearhart Mountain for fishing and a picnic on Tuesday. That's your early-release day, right? We have room for two more in the car. Would you two like to join us?"

Joey's lips pinch together, and I can tell he's all set to say no. The old Joey would've jumped at the chance for a picnic, but not this Joey. "Well . . ." he starts. And then his face kind of relaxes. He glances at me. "Are you going, Nellie?"

My heart does a little spin.

"You should come," Joey says.

An afternoon out with Joey, away from the twins, without chores or homework—I can't think of anything better. So what if I don't like sticking worms on hooks—who cares?

"Yes," I tell him, "yes."

"Wonderful, Nellie," the pastor says. "How about it then, Joey?"

"Well, I haven't been fishing in ages," he thinks out loud. "Yeah—I mean, yes. Thanks."

"Lovely," says the pastor. "We'll pick you up right around noon. We've got the food covered. But bring your own poles."

Mrs. Mitchell chimes in: "Thank you for serving our country today." She rests one hand on her growing belly, like she's protecting it from the war. I bet she hopes it's a girl.

When they leave, Joey goes back to work. I start clearing space for more salvage, smiling to myself about my good luck. What a morning—first I got to make Irene mad as a hornet, then I got to make plans to spend Tuesday with Joey. What more could I ask for?

"Hey, Joey," I say. "You been to church lately?"

"Naw."

"You ever gone fishing up on Gearhart?"

"Couple of times," he answers. "Last summer—Ow, dammit!"

"You okay?"

"Mm." He sucks on his finger, the one with his brother's school ring. "Just a little cut."

But it's not a little cut. It's a slice, much deeper than the one I got yesterday with the bread knife. He presses it shut, but blood still drips down his finger and over his brother's ring.

"Come sit over here." I point to the grass next to me. When I spot Ruby crossing the schoolyard with a pitcher, I call, "Hey, Rubes, can we get some water and a Band-Aid?"

She nods and holds up a just-a-minute finger.

"It's nothing," Joey says, refusing to sit.

"Maybe so, but you're gonna scare all the customers away if we don't get it cleaned up."

Ruby brings us a cup of iced tea and a first-aid kit. "Will this work? I'm due back in the kitchen now."

"That'll be fine. Set it down on the table, would you?"

I take off his brother's school ring and pop it in my pocket. Then I hand him the tea glass and tell him to stick his finger in. He still doesn't look happy about the unwanted attention, but he does as I ask.

"Ouch!" He jerks his finger out of the tea glass. "Jeepers creepers, is there lemon in this?"

"Oops, sorry, Joey. Hold it in there another second. Okay, you can take it out."

Now I see the gash. Not terrible, no stitches needed, but still ugly. I pat his finger dry with a piece of gauze from the first-aid kit and apply the bandage. "Press on it for a couple of minutes, make sure the bleeding stops."

"Yes, Nurse Doud." He's not trying to be funny. He's upset. Well, I can't help him with that right now. While he squeezes his finger and scowls, I busy myself with the next customer.

We still have an hour to go on the salvage drive. At noon, Mr. Shampine from the public works will come load everything we've collected into his truck and drive it to a place where it will get fashioned into things they can use at the front. Which is how we'll all get to send a little piece of ourselves over to where the fighting is happening.

I glance over at Joey and notice him looking at something over my shoulder. I turn around. It's Mr. DiNapoli, walking past with a megaphone in his hand. Mr. DiNapoli is the head of the volunteer fire department, and he's also been mayor since last fall. He's got a serious look on his usually jolly face, and he's walking fast. He goes straight to the middle of the street and plants himself there.

"Everyone, please gather around!" he shouts into the megaphone. "Gather around, would you?"

I go cold. The last time I got called to an assembly, our principal announced that President Roosevelt was dead. It was just a few weeks ago, all of us walking, practically running down to the gymnasium, thinking the war must be over, that we'd won, that our fathers and brothers were coming home. But then we saw the principal's face. Ruby and I caught hands. Had we been attacked? Were we losing Europe?

No. The President had died suddenly that afternoon. The

man who was supposed to win us the war, and cure polio, too, had left us. Mr. Harry Truman would step into office after only a handful of weeks as vice president.

And now here's Mr. DiNapoli, looking like he's holding a hot pepper on his tongue. Why should I rush over just to hear more grim news?

14

TAMIKO

November 21, 1944

Today the blue konnyaku glue reminds me of the sky. Everything reminds me of the sky, now that I see so little of it. I feel like a crab as I shuttle between my two washi boards, crawling sideways along a dark, sticky bottom. Where are the dried sardines and pickled radishes now? They're old memories.

Two rice balls a day aren't nearly enough to keep us going on twelve-hour shifts, sometimes longer. The handsome soldier reminds us that this is what the enemy makes us endure. This is why we must work as hard as we can. So I do. As hard as I can, and then harder still.

"I have to go to the bathroom," Suki whispers in my ear. I don't look up from my work. Suki has picked up a cough, and I'm afraid this is all too much for her. "Do you need a bathroom, or do you need a break?"

"What kind of break would the bathroom be?" she says.

She's right. The bathroom is freezing cold. Only this workroom is warm, and that's not for our sake. The hot steam-blasting machines are here to dry the washi.

"Go then," I tell her. "I'll watch your boards." We all watch each other's boards—because we'll all have to stay late if our table doesn't make quota.

Suki asks the handsome soldier for permission, then heads out. She's gone for a long time—at least, it feels that way—and we don't reach quota, so we have to stay an extra hour. When we're finally dismissed, there's yet another hardship to face. The steam blasters have made our clothes damp. As we march back to the dorm in the biting cold, the wind stabs like needles and makes icicles in our hair. We could freeze right here in the street, ice statues, and no one would notice until morning.

"Let's make sure we hit quota tomorrow," the girl called Rin says. We're all walking as fast as we can to get out of the cold. "Let's all work our utmost."

I lean in to Rin. "It's Suki's fault," I tell her. "She keeps going to the bathroom. I should know—I have to cover for her."

Rin glances over her shoulder to Suki, who's blowing her nose and coughing, then gives me a quick nod.

Now Suki catches up with Rin and me. She sniffles and hacks, and all at once Grandmother's words come back to me. The human tongue is sharper than the hornet's sting. I glance at Suki. I want to tell Rin that Suki is my closest friend. That I'm just hungry. And cold. And tired. Very, very tired. But I don't say anything. I just keep marching.

When we get to the dorm, we each get a bowl of plain miso soup and a little dish of gray rice with a piece of sweet potato. None of it has any flavor, but I spice it with the salt of my bridled tears. Tears from my fire-horse hip, from my frozen feet. Tears for the things I said about Suki. Tears for my starved belly. In a few minutes it will be lights-out, and I can't wait to escape into sleep.

But then something strange happens. As we finish up our food—it doesn't take us long to wolf it down—a soldier I don't recognize joins us. We stand up to greet him. Have we done something wrong?

The soldier, who reminds me a little bit of Kyo, doesn't look at us as he speaks. He focuses on the opposite wall and announces, "Sleep well tonight, workers. Sleep as long as you wish. You won't be awakened for the six a.m. shift."

The room is silent. Have we failed our great Emperor? Will we be sent home in shame?

"You must think of this as a holiday," the soldier adds. "As a gift from his Imperial Majesty. A chance to store up sleep and strength."

Suki sighs. So do I. We all do. We sigh and smile and squeeze each other's hands. Sleep. A holiday. A gift from His Majesty. I'm so delighted, I don't even notice the soldier leaving until he switches the lights off on his way. And just like that, it's time to begin our long sleep.

Lying on my mat tonight, my body curled into a ball, my little cotton blanket tight around my legs, I think of blue skies and potato chips and warm summer days. I think of Kyo and victory and poor lonely Auntie. I think of Suki and how badly she needs this rest. Then I fall into a long, deep sleep.

Most of us sleep until noon. A few of the girls are still snoring into the afternoon. It's cold inside the dorm, but not as cold as the outdoors, and we're thrilled to laze around on our mats all day. We each do our best to make our single rice ball last, to make our tongues find flavor where there is none, to make our bellies feel satisfaction where there is still hunger.

Suki and I lie on our backs and talk about the victory to come, about the peace ahead, about returning to our families. We're ravenous, and our muscles feel like jelly, but we're determined to enjoy the holiday our Emperor has given us.

In the late afternoon, the soldier from last night reappears, rubbing his hands together and looking wind-burned. It must be extra cold out today. We stand.

"Workers," he says to the wall. "Today we change shifts. Starting today, and for the next two weeks, you will work from six p.m. to six a.m."

Murmurs ripple through the hallway. I think back to our first morning at work here, how we watched the older girls leave the theater after toiling all night. Now it's our turn to be the owls. Well, this is good. Owls bring luck. Owls protect. This will be our lucky shift . . . I hope.

The soldier opens his rucksack and extracts a paper bag. "Here." He sets the bag on the floor. "Some sweet potato. Be at the theater by five forty-five."

As soon as he's out of the room, we dive into the bruised slices of what were once sun-sweetened roots.

It's strange to start your workday at the time you're used to ending it. But we've had a rice ball and some sweet potato and a day of resting, so we have energy to work. Rin has gained a little color in her cheeks, and Suki hasn't coughed in half an hour.

Maybe we'll make quota on time tonight. Maybe this is just what we needed. I feel almost happy. At the start, anyway.

After a few hours, my eyes droop, and my finger hurts. No one at our table is working very fast, even though the handsome soldier keeps calling out for everyone to "produce, produce!" We're normally fast asleep by this hour. We can't fool our bodies into believing it's daytime. Besides, we're hungry again.

Then at midnight something unexpected happens. The handsome soldier appears on the stage and calls out, "You may break now!"

I'm not sure I heard him right. "Did he say . . . ?" I ask Suki. She nods. "I think so."

Rin agrees.

Then another soldier enters through the back door carrying boxes of—Could it be? Yes, rice balls! We almost swoon with delight. This makes the night shift worth it.

When he reaches the front of the room, the soldier says, "One rice ball per worker."

We quickly line up. The soldier hands each girl something else after she takes her rice ball.

"What is that?" I ask my friends, but they don't know. None of us knows.

Finally, it's my turn. I reach into the box for the treasure. The rice balls are smaller than usual, but they're something. Then the soldier drops a white tablet into my hand.

"Another gift from the Emperor," the soldier tells me. Medicine, from the Emperor? I eye the tablet. But I'm not sick. What will it do to me? Should I save it in case I do get sick?

Maybe I should give it to Suki, for her cold.

"Just take it," the soldier says.

So I do. We all do. We stand around gobbling our rice balls and swallowing the pills. Within five minutes, we're back at our washi tables. Funny, we don't get one bit sleepy the whole rest of the night. Or the nights after that. After a week, there are no more midnight rice balls, but now we get two white tablets.

15
NELLIE
May 2, 1945

I don't go over to Mr. DiNapoli and his megaphone. I'm staying right here at the tin station. I don't want to know who died or what other calamity has struck. But then Joey says, "C'mon, Nellie," so I finally do. There must be fifty or more people standing around. I can't find Ruby to hold on to, and I can't possibly grab Joey's hand, so I fold my arms against my chest and brace myself.

"I'm sorry to interrupt this important drive," Mr. DiNapoli says. "But I want you all to know that Adolf Hitler is dead! Put a gun to his head. The Nazis are expected to surrender within days."

The crowd is silent for a fraction of a second. Someone laughs as if to test the waters. Then we all erupt into every happy sound imaginable—cheers and shouts and yowls and tears. I jump as high as I can, my arms to the sky. Because Adolf Hitler is dead. Because the Nazis are expected to surrender within days. I jump and jump and jump.

Peace! my pounding heart cries out. Victory! And above it all, Pa! I'm happier than I've ever felt. It's the most amazing moment of my life. I never want it to end. Mr. DiNapoli dances with Mrs. Flynn right there in the middle of the street. Someone starts belting out "Swing Out to Victory," and we all join in. Everyone is singing and laughing and having a ball.

No, not everyone. Not Joey. Maybe he thinks Hitler got off too easy. Maybe he wanted to shoot Hitler himself. Maybe it's just too hard for Joey to be around so many happy people. I don't know. He used to tell me what he was thinking, but now I just have to guess. And what I'm guessing is, he's furious with the whole world.

"Folks," Mr. DiNapoli says, trying to catch his breath. "Folks . . . folks!" The crowd goes quiet. "Remember now, this is not the end of the war. Our men are still battling Japan in the South Pacific. But this is the best news we could have asked for."

The whoops rise up again. Mrs. Engen whoops because her oldest boy will finally be coming home from Europe. Mr. Swanson whoops because his grandson won't have to get called up. Mr. Kava whoops because he won't have to send any more boys off to war. And I whoop too. Because we're winning the war. Because Pa is one step closer to coming home. It's like Christmas and Thanksgiving and the Fourth of July all rolled into one.

I look over to Joey and remember that for him it's Memorial Day, too. I feel awful for him. But I'm still over the moon.

The next thing I know, Joan Patzke is next to me instead

of Joey. She takes both my hands, and we jump up and down together.

"It's over!" she shouts. "Hitler is over!"

I remember how Joan and I used to jump rope together at recess, how we always jumped and laughed and made ourselves dizzy, back when we were younger. Now here we are, doing it again. It's perfect.

I can't remember how the celebration or the salvage drive end, only that I catch sight of Joey stepping into his father's car for another day at the farm. Then Ruby finds me and we run all the way home. When we get to her house, her grandpa is sitting on his front porch rocker, the brim of his hat covering his eyes and half his nose. He's grinning like a pig in slop, the front door open and the wireless turned up full blast. The radio announcer over in Lakeview reads from a wire report:

Again, the German radio has announced that Adolf Hitler fell yesterday afternoon as Berlin burned. We repeat, Hitler has fallen. His capital has crumbled. His vision of world domination has vanished.

Ruby's grandpa doesn't even know we're here until the radio switches to a commercial. Then he comes to. "We always beat 'em," he says, because he fought the Germans in the First World War. "Let's hope they learned their lesson this time."

Then he does a strange thing. He gets up off his rocker, walks over to the side of the house, and opens the door to his aviary. He doesn't go inside, though, just stands there with his backside holding the door open. When nothing happens, he says, "Go on now, gals. I'm setting you free. Go wherever you like."

But they don't fly off. One of them hops over to his feet and kind of pecks at the dirt, that's all. He gives them another minute or two, then leaves the door ajar. "Damn fools," he mutters on his way into the house.

Fools? Seems to me the birds have a pretty good thing going here. All the food they can eat, a safe place to sleep, a doting owner. Why would they want to bother with rain and wind and foxes and tomcats? Just because a person—or a bird—can do something doesn't mean they want to, or should, does it?

When I get to my house, Henry and Willie are marching around our yard with their American flags, singing "Boogie Woogie Bugle Boy" at the top of their voices. They have soup pots on their heads like army helmets, and their T-shirts are hanging out of their shorts. They look silly, but I'm in too good a mood to care. When they spot me, they come running. "Victory! Did you hear? Victory for us!"

I tap their pot-tops like drums and sing, "You're the boogie woogie boogeymen of Company D," which cracks them up.

Inside, Mrs. Wells sits in the kitchen with Mother, who has splurged and poured coffee with full servings of sugar and milk. Mrs. Wells is bright-eyed and smiling. Mother just looks relieved, like two or three trees from her forest of worry have fallen.

"Nellie, did the boys tell you?" she asks.

"We heard at the drive."

"Isn't it wonderful news?" Mrs. Wells says. "I was telling your mother we should throw a party."

"And I was telling Mrs. Wells," says Mother, "that no one can give a party on rations. Oh wait, quiet, everyone." She leans over to turn up the volume on the wireless.

They're reading Hitler's obituary. I lean against the kitchen counter and listen. They take us through his whole life, and at the end they tell us about his personal habits. How he liked to sit in the front of the car with the chauffeur instead of in the back. How he didn't like jewelry. How he was a poor sleeper and ate lunch at precisely two o'clock every day. I don't like this last part. It's like they're making him out to be a human being.

When the obituary is over, Mother asks, "How was the salvage drive?" Which is more interest than she usually shows in me these days. Ding-dong, Hitler is dead, and maybe Mother is coming to life.

"Good," I say. "Pastor and Mrs. Mitchell came by and invited me to a picnic Tuesday over on Gearhart. Said they could pick me up."

"Can the boys go too?"

"Sorry, no extra room in the car." Thankfully.

"And how was Mrs. Mitchell looking?" asks Mrs. Wells. "Dotty, you know she's with child."

"She looked fine," I say.

"Is she starting to . . . ?" Mrs. Wells mimics a big belly with her hands. I nod.

"Well, how nice."

Then the twins scuttle into the kitchen, all hot and flushed, looking for a snack. I head upstairs to change into shorts—which is when I realize I still have Joey's brother's ring in my trouser pocket. I suppose I could drop it off with his mother right now, so it's waiting for him when he gets back from the farm. But I think I'll let him come over here to get it himself. Then maybe our hands will brush. Maybe our fingers will kiss. Maybe we'll be friends again. Or even something more than friends.

Yup, today has been absolutely perfect.

16
TAMIKO
December 12, 1944

Ancestors,

No pen or paper here, so I must write this letter in my head. I've been at the theater for a month now. Auntie was right. She warned me to be careful what I wish for. Sensei was right too. It's not anything at all like I imagined.

A theater isn't magic when the costumes and the lights are gone, when the actors and the audience are replaced by girls toiling over tables, when you labor there twelve hours each day, Suki on my left, Rin on my right. The air is stale, the floors are hard, our eyes are waning moons. Everything is tired—fingers, feet, lungs.

Worst of all, they lied when they said the food would be plentiful here. We haven't had a decent meal since our first day of work. The only abundance here is misery and sweat, second helpings for all.

I know we must sacrifice ourselves for our nation, for our Emperor. But I don't know how much more we have left to give. I hope Auntie is faring better than I am. I hope Kyo is still alive.

~ *Tamiko*

I stand at the washi table, barefoot, working. Sheet over sheet, next to sheet, next to sheet. Slapping the konnyaku potato glue, brushing out the bubbles. All day or all night, depending on the shift. We must produce. We must glue.

I do produce. I do glue.

Suki keeps coughing, practically barking, and Rin wilts, ready to faint. My fingers ache and my hip flames. Every withered belly in the theater mewls in pain. Still, we produce.

"What are you thinking about?" Suki whispers. "Hmm?" I say.

"You have that look in your eyes. You're far away."

I slap glue onto my rack. "I'm thinking about the ikiryō."

"The what?"

"Ikiryō. My father told me stories about them. When he worked in the garden, weeding the cabbage sprouts. Ikiryō are spirits that escape the body and travel around."

She puts her hand to her mouth and coughs. "Why on earth are you thinking about that?"

"Because. Because I'd like to become an ikiryō. Anything to escape my hunger."

"Did your father tell you how to set your spirit loose?"

I add another layer of washi paper to my rack. "I never asked. I thought it was a fairy tale."

"I'm so tired of paper," Suki sighs. "I even dream about it. Origami paper. Calligraphy paper. Gift wrap."

"Paper dolls?" I ask. "Kites? Books?"

Suki nods. "And the tōrō nagashi."

I go quiet. The gliding paper lanterns are for grieving.

Suddenly, I wonder how many lanterns I'll need to make by the time this war ends. Will Kyo's name be on one of them? How many other mourners will join me by the riverbank to set our beacons afloat? Or maybe Auntie will need to send my own name bobbing into the sunset. Maybe I'll starve to death here at the washi table.

But no. I won't let myself starve. I won't let Suki or Rin starve either.

We've been slapping the konnyaku glue for a month now. Slap, spread, slap. The paste we use here is gray and ugly, like this theater, but it reminds me of something else. It reminds me of the konnyaku root jellies and noodles dear Auntie used to make, wonderfully sweet and savory, back when there was food. And that memory, that lovely, faraway memory, gives me an idea. A wicked, wonderful idea.

I dip one finger into the potato glue. Look over both shoulders. Glance at Suki and Rin, who work with their heads down. Then I put my finger to my mouth. I eat the paste. Only a nibble from my cracked and blistered finger. Then a morsel more. No flavor, no aroma, just something to chew, to trick my belly and my mind.

Rin sees what I'm doing. She grimaces. "Tamiko, no," she mouths.

"Try it," I urge.

She shakes her head.

"Just a little, Rin." I touch my belly. "To keep you going."

I can see the doubt in her face. She bites her lip, studies her drying board, and finally dips her finger into the glue. Just a taste, smaller than a pea, but it makes her cheeks glow pink.

"Suki, look," I whisper. She's busy gluing, but she looks up. I slyly put a bit of konnyaku on my tongue. "Lunch."

She looks to Rin and back to me. Something starts to form at the corners of her mouth—a smile perhaps, or a scolding, or maybe just another cough. Then she does it too. She feeds herself.

"Remember, Suki?" I say under my breath. "Remember my aunt's konnyaku noodles?"

"After school." Now she does smile. "Or in summer. In seaweed soup."

We're giddy at first, the three of us, revived. But this quickly rots into shame. What are we doing, stealing supplies? What if the balloons are for making food drops? Food to the cities, to the countryside, to little squealing boys and wise old aunts? Will our eating make them go hungry?

This is wrong.

I can tell from their frowns that Suki and Rin think the same thing, that this is bad. But we don't stop. We keep dipping our fingers in and chewing, telling ourselves that starving workers can't make balloons, and without balloons, how can food be dropped?

17

NELLIE

May 2, 1945

It's late, but I'm still up. It has just finished raining, and I'm lying on my bed humming "Boogie Woogie Bugle Boy" to myself and turning Joey's ring over and over in my hand.

When I hear tapping at the window, I think it's the rain starting up again. No—it's louder than rain. I lift my head and look out, but of course I don't see anything in the blackout. Now it sounds like pebbles pelting the pane. I get up and open the window. Joey is standing below with Poppy panting at his side. He's in shorts and a T-shirt, and I can just make out his eyes in the thin moonlight.

"Hey Joey," I say, but quietly, because everyone else in the house is probably asleep. "Your ring, right?"

"Yeah. Sorry it's late."

"That's okay. I'll be right down."

Outside, the wind is blowing away the rain clouds, and the air is full of cricket songs and jasmine perfume. I hand Joey the ring, which is hot from my clenched fist, and our hands brush again.

The grass is wet on my bare toes, sending a delicious chill up my legs.

"Thanks." He puts it on. "For a minute there, I thought I lost it."

"Yeah, sorry. It completely slipped my mind."

"Mine too. What a morning, huh?"

Poppy presses herself against my leg, and I scratch her head. "Maybe this will be the last salvage drive we'll ever have to run. Maybe the war is really going to end."

"Yeah. Too bad it took this long." He twirls his brother's ring around his finger.

"Joey—"

"Better late than never though, right?" He digs his hands into his jeans pockets and kicks the grass with his loafer. "Hey, remember back when it all started? I'd never heard of Pearl Harbor before."

"I had to ask my pa what *infamy* meant."

Joey raises his eyebrows.

"Mr. Roosevelt called it a day that will go down in infamy," I say.

"Oh, right. And I thought it would all be over by the end of the week. We'd join the war and the Allies would clean up."

"Jeepers, we were young," I muse.

"Remember that birthday cake my ma made me the first year under rationing?" he goes on. "It was supposed to be chocolate, I think. She made it from breadcrumbs. It didn't even go in the oven."

"Yeah, and how about that cartoon they used to show before

the movies?" I add. "The one where Minnie Mouse is frying bacon and Pluto wants the drippings."

Joey puts on his best Mickey Mouse voice. "Bacon grease makes glycerin. Glycerin makes explosives. Help win the war— donate your drippings to your local Fat Collection Station. That one?"

"Yup." I laugh.

But Joey isn't laughing back. He isn't even smiling. He has turned inward again—I can see it in his eyes. I wish I could reach in and pull him out, but I don't know how.

Joey lowers his chin. "My brother and I, we used to thumb a ride to the movies on Friday nights a lot. That's how I know the Mickey ditty by heart."

"Uh . . . yeah." I already know about the hitchhiking, doesn't he remember? Did he really forget that when his brother was alive, Joey told me most everything?

"*Son of Dracula,* that was his favorite," he says. "I think he liked the idea of living forever, y'know? Couldn't settle for sixty or seventy years like the rest of us."

"Maybe he—"

"Anyway," he interrupts, "thanks for bandaging up my finger."

Guess he's done talking about Peter. "Thanks for sticking up for me to Irene."

He opens his mouth, then shrugs.

I wish he'd tell me about the fire. Then it wouldn't be his secret, it would be our secret. But he's not telling me. He's standing right here in front of me, and even though we're talking, it feels like he's on the other side of the world.

"I'll let you get back inside," he says.

"Yeah, okay." Maybe I should tell him I know. Maybe it would be a relief for him to have someone to share the truth with. Or maybe it wouldn't. Maybe he'd resent how I followed him that night, how I spied.

I'm about to say good night when all at once I hear footsteps on the road. Running steps. It's Ruby, panting like the dog at my side.

She stops short when she spots me. With Joey. At this hour. In the dark. She starts to back up.

"Fancy seeing you here, Ruby," I say. "C'mon over."

She hesitates for a second, then walks over, her eyes darting between Joey and me. "Hi."

"Everything all right?" I know it isn't, of course, or she wouldn't be showing up like this.

"Well, I . . ." She glances at Joey again. "There's something in the aviary. Gramps must not've shut the door tight after he tried letting the doves out today."

"Something?" I ask.

She nods. "I heard noises, so I came downstairs and looked out the back. I'm not sure what it is—it's too dark—but it's big. Makes a terrible racket, too."

"Did it get the birds?" I ask.

"I don't know." Ruby's voice climbs. "I thought maybe you could help me, y'know, look."

"Um, okay."

"I'll go too," Joey says.

"Really?" we both ask.

"Sure," he says. "Let me just bring Poppy home."

I run inside to grab my shoes. When I get back out, Joey is coming down his driveway holding a flashlight.

"What about the blackout?" Ruby says.

Joey raises his head to the sky. "You see any kamikazes around?"

We don't answer.

"Me either. C'mon," he says. "I'll only light it for a second. Just to see what we're dealing with."

Ruby whispers in my ear, "You don't think Irene Kava could be right, do you?"

"About what?"

"About the Japanese coming back from the camps. About revenge."

"I don't know . . . I mean, no. I mean . . . do you?"

She shrugs. "Someone's in the aviary. Someone or something. And they sound like they mean war."

Ruby is right about the racket. We can hear the growling or barking or whatever it's doing before we even make it around to the side of the house. Ruby's grandpa must be a sound sleeper to snooze through this.

The aviary is really only a cage made of chicken wire and some wood slats. We stop about twenty feet away. In the back corner, we see a black silhouette huddling—or maybe it's crouching. There are no bird sounds, no bird movement, no bird shadows, just the outline of this beast in the moonlight. Now that Joey has put *Son of Dracula* into my head, I think of every horror movie I've ever seen or heard of. I want to shriek. I want to run away. I want *Bambi*.

"How many birds were there, anyway?" Joey whispers.

"A dozen or so, I guess," Ruby says.

"All right, I'm gonna turn the light on. Do you two want to wait inside?"

I'm pretty sure I don't want to see what's in there, not the intruder and not whatever it has done to the doves. But Ruby shakes her head, so we're staying. Joey takes a couple of steps closer, raises his flashlight, and turns it on.

There it is, bigger and darker than I could have imagined. I clap my hand to my mouth. Joey jumps back, dropping the flashlight and almost crashing into me. I don't know if we're looking at a Japanese American or a wildcat. A bear or even Sasquatch himself. All I know is, they're mad.

18

TAMIKO

January 30, 1945

Suki starts coughing, and that's nothing new. But now she steps away from her gluing boards and bends over, barking and hacking and gasping for air.

"Suki?" I rub her back.

Rin kneels in front of her. "Suki, we're here."

Suki is quiet for a few seconds, her face as gray as the konnyaku glue. When she hacks again, she coughs up blood. This isn't just a cold, a sniffle. This is something much worse.

The other girls at our table jump back. The girls at the table next to us stop working and stare. Soon the whole auditorium stops working. All eyes are on Suki. The silence screams in my ears.

Suki needs a place to lie down, but not here, not on the hard floor caked in glue. I look to the stage for our handsome soldier, but he isn't there. I look all around the auditorium, but no soldier.

"Rin, you stay with her," I say. "I'll be right back."

Rin's eyes grow wide. "Tamiko, no. We're not allowed to leave the auditorium without permission, you know that." But Suki is my best friend, and she needs me. She needs me the way I needed her during the long march to Kure City, the way I needed her that first cold night here. I can't stand here and watch her suffer.

"I'm giving myself permission." I run to the door at the back of the auditorium.

I can feel Rin's eyes on the back of my head, begging me to come back. I can feel all the other girls at all the other tables trying not to look, not to gape at the girl who dares walk away from her work.

I open the door and step into the lobby. The far wall features a mural of a giant samurai warrior stomping on Allied ships and crushing their planes. The handsome soldier stands against that wall, talking to another soldier. They don't notice me.

"The bombs are prepared and waiting," I hear the other soldier say.

"Good," the handsome soldier says. "The balloons are almost ready for assembly."

My heart was already throbbing, but now it hammers in my chest. Bombs. Balloons. What does it mean? Is that what we're making—something that will drop bombs, not food?

Now the other soldier notices me and the handsome soldier turns around. They both scowl at the disobedient girl who has abandoned her washi table.

I don't venture too close. "Forgive me," I say from halfway across the lobby. "One of my comrades is very ill. Coughing blood. Please."

The handsome soldier doesn't waste a moment. He runs past me into the auditorium. I follow close behind. By the time I get through the door, he's already at Suki's side.

We all watch the handsome soldier help Suki straighten up. She lets him steer her to the back door, even though she doesn't know where he's taking her. The rest of us stand in our spots, meek as abandoned cats. Where is she going? Does she know I'm right here—right here for her, for whatever she needs? She walks past me without seeing me.

As soon as the door closes behind them, the auditorium fills with whispers.

"Kekkaku," the girls mutter.

Tuberculosis? Now I'm twice as terrified for Suki. I'm terrified for myself too, thinking of the blanket we shared. Of the radish I stole. Of all the hours and hours I've stood next to her while we worked. I realize I'm wringing my hands, as if I'm washing them with invisible soap. Tuberculosis is the sickness of war, and I blame the Americans. They're the ones who starve us, who attack us, who take my brother and my best friend away from me. We must defeat them, and soon.

I stop wrenching my hands long enough to look around our worktable. "Are you all right?" I ask Rin. Her hair has been falling out for days, strand by strand, like ebony embroidery threads.

Rin nods. "And you?"

I look down at my cracked and blistered fingers, ruined for the needle. Ruined for anything but gluing washi. I take a halting breath. "I'll be all right, as long as Suki is okay."

The theater door opens and the handsome soldier reappears,

alone. He shouts across the auditorium, "Don't worry about your comrade. She has served our nation and our Emperor well."

What does that mean? It means Suki won't return to work, yes. But I want to know more. I want to know where Suki is right now. Where she'll go. Who will take her there. When I can see her—if I can see her. Suddenly, I feel completely alone, even with all of these girls around me, like a grain of sand blown onto an unfamiliar beach.

My throat starts to burn, and I wonder if I'm getting sick too. I think I'd like that—then perhaps Suki and I could go home together. But no, that's wrong. That's absurd. I swallow hard, forcing down my selfish thoughts.

The handsome soldier takes a few steps forward. "You have all worked hard with us these last two months," he says. "Now your labor is almost complete. You will all be going home by week's end."

Going home. We'll be going home by week's end.

Excited chatter buzzes and rumbles around me, the noise of relief, of gladness. I see more smiles in this moment than I've seen in all the weeks we've been here. My comrades are all calling out the same word: home. I can see it on their lips, but I can't hear it. I can only hear the panic of Suki's choking cough, the tick of waiting bombs. Louder, closer, realer every second. For once, I don't feel hunger, and I wonder if I'm already sick.

"You have served our Emperor honorably," the handsome soldier goes on. "Now you must get back to work. Make the most of your last hours here."

The talking quiets down but doesn't disappear. I return to my washi boards, Rin on my right, Suki's shadow on my left. Slap and paste, slap and paste, as fast as ever. I do it for Suki's recovery, for Kyo's survival, for victory. My poor Suki!

While I work, I'm haunted—not by ghosts, but by myself, by the terrible person I've become. A person who'd steal her best friend's food, who'd blame her for a missed quota, who'd envy her for her good fortune. Suki would never, ever treat me like that. She'd share her blanket. She'd help me hide my limp on a long march. She'd remind me how to toss a coin at the kami shrine. I was so stupid.

Maybe I still am stupid. Stupid enough to leave my washi rack for the second time this morning. I can't help it. I can't stand here not knowing if Suki will come home with the rest of us. Or if she'll ever come home. I can't glue another sheet until I find out.

"Watch my boards," I tell Rin.

Striding toward the handsome soldier at the back of the auditorium, I keep my eyes on the far wall, not on him. If I dared look his way, his scowl might make me turn and run back to my washi board. I focus instead on a spot just above his head.

I stop a few paces away from him. I haven't stood this close to him since our training session back in the dorm building, back when I took my turn gluing sheets of paper. He didn't look me in the eye then, but he does now, and his face is perfectly unreadable. Does he pity me for losing Suki or despise me for abandoning my work?

I gaze at him now, trying to summon my words, but something happens to him—or maybe to me. He's not there. I blink to clear my vision, but he's gone. In his place stands my brother! At least, that's how it seems. It's Kyo, with his short-clipped soldier's hair and his warm brown eyes peeking out from his cap. Kyo, standing so close to me, as if he knew I needed him. His presence enfolds me like the softest wings of the downiest swan.

And then an icy thought grips me by the throat. Is this Kyo's ghost? Has he perished in battle?

"Kyo?" I try to say, but nothing comes out.

"Are you ill?" The handsome soldier is back. Kyo is gone. I shake my head.

"Then what is it?" His voice is neither hard nor tender.

I clear my throat and manage a croaky, "Suki."

He inspects my face for a long moment. I want to disappear like the steam from a hot cup of tea. Finally, he pushes the auditorium door open and nods for me to follow him out. He leads me to a corner of the lobby, drills his eyes into mine, clasps his hands behind his back, and speaks. "Your comrade will be taken to her home today."

I close my eyes and let out a long breath. They wouldn't release a worker home early unless she was gravely ill. When I open my eyes, the soldier has taken a step back.

"Is that all?" he asks.

"Yes. No."

He frowns.

"Sir, you say our work is almost finished. Can you tell me then, what has it all been for?" I didn't plan to say this. It's not my place. The words simply slip from my mouth, like hatchlings pecking their way out of the egg.

The soldier's eyebrows fall into an angry line.

"I'd like to be able to tell Suki," I add quickly. "I'd like her to know what she's worked so hard for. What she has endured this illness for."

Still he says nothing. Maybe he wants to make me squirm. Maybe he wants to make sure no one else has wandered over. When he finally speaks, his voice is low, and I must lean in to hear him.

"The ten thousand balloons will carry ten thousand bombs to America," he says.

Ten thousand bombs to America. To the land that starves us and kills our brothers. To the nation that bombs our cities. Ten thousand bombs to America.

"The bombs will explode wherever they land," he goes on. "All across America, they will kill, burn, terrorize."

"And end this terrible war?" I ask. "And bring my brother—our brothers—home to us?"

"Exactly so."

Suddenly, I'm dizzy with awe. These balloons we toil over, they'll bring Kyo home. They'll bring food to Auntie's table. They'll bring peace. I'm so astonished, I think the floor is going to fly up and hit me in the face.

"Do you need air?" he asks.

I shake my head.

"Good. Because I have a task for you."

"Sir?"

"You were brave enough to ask me about the balloons. I choose you to share the news with your comrades."

I look over my shoulder at the auditorium door. "There are many comrades," I say.

"Go to the stage and tell them all."

"Me?" I say, my breath catching.

"Do it now, so you can get back to your washi table."

After I bow, I return to the auditorium and climb the steps onto the front stage. Rin is the only one who notices. She looks afraid for me.

"Comrades," I say. My voice sounds loud in my ears, but only the girls in the front can hear me. "Comrades!" I shout.

Now everyone looks at me. Stares, really. They cannot believe I've dared to interrupt their work. They glance at the handsome soldier standing against the back wall. They're waiting for him to drag me off the stage. He doesn't.

"Comrades," I repeat. "I've been asked to share good news with you."

Whispers stir the air.

I raise my hand for quiet. "The balloons we're building here—they will carry ten thousand bombs to America. They'll help us win the war. Bring peace. Achieve the universal brotherhood. The eight corners of the world under one roof."

Now the whispers explode into cheers. I look across the auditorium to the handsome soldier, and he nods.

"Comrades," I say. "We must return to our work. The bombs are waiting."

I climb down the stairs and go back to my table. To slap and paste, slap and paste. I do it because Suki is sick, because Kyo is risking his life, because we're all so hungry and working so hard. For the first time in this place, I smile.

19

NELLIE

May 2, 1945

I'm ready to bolt from the enemy in the aviary. I think Joey is too. But not Ruby. She marches straight over to the brute.

"Gramps?" she says.

What?

"Huh?" her grandpa grumbles from the back corner of the aviary, where he has been snoring to wake the dead. "That you, Ruby?"

"Gramps, what's the matter?" Ruby runs to him, with Joey lighting the way. "We thought there was a beast in here. What's wrong?"

"Shhh, nothing. Look." He points to the house.

"I don't see anything," she says.

"Boy there, with the flashlight," he calls. "Who is that?"

"Joey Cooper, sir."

"The Cooper boy, eh? All right, well, shine it up at my bedroom—the top window there."

Joey does as he's told, and now we see. The doves are nestled on the windowsill, asleep.

"Gramps?"

"They wouldn't want to leave when I tried to let them go today," he gripes. "Not only that, they wanted to get even closer to me. Gathered right outside my window and made a regular ruckus. I thought I could coax them back in here, but I guess we all fell asleep instead."

I want to laugh but force myself not to.

"Nice to know I still have some friends left in this world," he goes on, gazing up at the birds.

"You've got plenty of friends," Ruby says, "starting with the three of us. Come on, Nellie and Joey. Time to put some birds to bed."

Joey and I trade glances. "How?" I ask.

"You stay right here, Gramps." Ruby motions us to follow her into the house.

We go through the back door into the tiny kitchen. She fills three tall glasses with water and hands us each one. "Doves hate getting wet."

She leads us up the staircase, down a short hall, into her grandpa's room, which is just big enough for a bed, a small chest of drawers, and a beat-up trunk. "Okay, when I open the window, douse the birds and make as much noise as you can. Ready?"

We crowd around the single window.

"One, two, three!"

We all act like maniacs, throwing water and yelling and making a hubbub. The birds are not pleased. They fuss and flap their wings and fly off the sill.

"Look out below!" Ruby calls.

Amazingly, the plan works. By the time we drop our glasses by the kitchen sink and get outside, Ruby's grandpa is latching the gate on his flock. "Bunch of lunatic hens," he mutters. "Thanks for the help, kids."

"Come on, Gramps," Ruby urges. "It's getting cold out."

He yawns. "You coming too?"

"In just a minute," she says.

When the back door slaps behind him, I finally allow myself a laugh out loud. "That was nuts."

"That's my Gramps."

I shake my head. "I still can't tell whether he loves those birds or hates them."

"Both," Ruby says. "The same way he feels about me."

I stop laughing.

"Don't worry, Nelly Bly, it's fine. Like Gramps says, your nearest and dearest are also the biggest pains in the arse 'cause you gotta worry about them all the time, that's all."

"You're smarter than you look, Rubes."

"Ha-ha. Anyway, I should get inside," she says. "I'll see ya. And thanks. You too, Joey."

Joey and I walk back up the road, the two of us under a billion brilliant stars. What if we weren't just heading home from Ruby's? What if we were out for a secret late-night stroll, and he had a sparkly new bracelet in his pocket for me . . . and then we'd have our first kiss? I'm so lost in my dream, I'd probably walk right past my own house, except that Joey stops at the foot of my driveway.

"Well, mission accomplished," he says. The moonlight makes his flushed cheeks glimmer.

"Good teamwork."

He nods. Takes a small step closer. Parts his lips. Leans in.

My belly somersaults, and I can't breathe.

"That was kind of fun," he whispers, then steps back.

No kiss. Still, the way his words tickle my ear, it feels like one. "Y-yeah."

"Well, see ya."

"Yup, see ya, Joey."

I linger in the yard until I hear his screen door screech open and clang shut. Then I lie on the wet grass and look up at the night sky, admiring the quarter moon, finding the constellations, imagining the stars are spelling out victory.

Then I see movement. What is that sailing by? Another shooting star! Ahhh . . . a perfect ending to a perfect day.

Wait a minute . . . what is that thing up there, really? It doesn't have the plume or the glow of a shooting star—it's only reflecting the moonlight. And it doesn't have the arc of a falling star—it's drifting, zigzagging, bobbing. Then it disappears behind—or maybe it lands on—Gearhart Mountain to the north. It's probably not really a shooting star, but I make a wish on it anyway. Just in case.

I wake up early the next morning, even earlier than on a school day. A dream jolted me awake, I think, a dream about . . . I don't remember what. Not that it matters. I stay in bed awhile longer, thinking about how perfect yesterday was, thinking about the thing I saw floating near Gearhart Mountain, thinking maybe I'll slip back into another dream. But I don't. Instead, I watch the twilight dissolve into dawn and the shadows sharpen into colors. Then I get up to slice bread.

The twins are already downstairs, kneeling over a marble game on the living room floor. Willie accuses Henry of cheating, and Henry blames Willie for breaking his shooter. I tiptoe past them.

Mother has left a cookbook on the table. It's Betty Crocker's *Your Share*, a booklet about wartime cooking, open to the section on entertaining. I page through it. For a barbecue, it suggests writing the invitations on paper bags and telling guests to use the bags to bring their own hot dog or burger patty. For a hobo party, you're supposed to use tin plates and "hand out" peanut butter sandwiches. Is Mother really thinking about throwing a party? No, not yet. Not before Pa comes home. I hope he comes home soon.

I call the twins in for breakfast. "Will you take us to Best Novelties today?" Henry asks, skidding across the floor onto his chair.

"Can't."

"Why not?"

"No money."

"We just wanna look," Henry says, mouth full of buttered toast.

"Well, I have a ton of homework."

"But—"

"Hey, Ruby's grandpa tried to let his doves go yesterday," I say, just to change the subject.

"Let them go?" Willie asks. "Go where?"

"Wherever they wanted. To the other side of the world if they felt like it. But they wouldn't budge."

"I wish I could fly," Willie sighs. "If I had wings, I'd never come down, not even for lunch."

"We'll take them!" Henry gushes. "If Ruby's grandpa doesn't want them anymore, we'll take care of them."

"I don't think that's what Ruby's grandpa had in mind," I tell them. "He wanted to set them free, not move their cage down the road a few houses."

The twins look puzzled, but they don't argue the point. They drop their empty plates into the sink and run outside to get themselves in trouble—saving me from having to explain that Mother would never, ever let them keep a bunch of birds, not even if they came delivered on a silver platter.

After I wash the dishes, I head upstairs to attack that pile of homework. I open my geography notebook and try to memorize the waterways of Canada. But I don't absorb much. I'm too busy waiting for Tuesday's picnic. To an afternoon up on the mountain in high spring, an afternoon with Joey. I wonder if it will be the day I get my best friend back . . . or more. I say a little prayer that it will be.

20
TAMIKO
February 6, 1945

All the washi has been glued and sent for assembly. All the schoolgirls have been dismissed from the theater, like actors after the closing show. All the cotton sleeping mats have been rolled up and set aside. It's time to go home.

The handsome soldier doesn't come to see us off. Instead, a new soldier arrives to walk us back to Shinji-cho. We cover our thin bodies with our thin blankets and start trudging. We're cold and hungry, but we hold our heads high. We've helped make the balloons that will carry the bombs to America and help end this terrible war. As we tromp on, I don't even try to hide my limp.

When I walk into our cottage, my hip screaming, Auntie doesn't look surprised. She looks horrified. There were no mirrors at the washi factory, but I know how I look. I look like all the other girls there.

"Where is the rest of you?" she asks as she holds me.

I want to laugh, but I'm too tired. "Is there any word of Kyo?"

Instead of answering, she hugs me a little tighter.

"Auntie?" My heart is in my throat.

"No, my dear, no word."

No, of course there's no word. There was hardly any word even when he was at the training camp. Now he's out fighting. At least we haven't received a death report. At least there's that.

"The war will end soon," I tell her.

She walks me to the low table. "That's what I pray for every day."

"No, I mean truly." I kneel on my cushion. My beautiful, soft cushion. "The army is sending ten thousand bombs to America."

"Why do you think this, Tamiko?"

"Because that's what we were doing in Kure City."

Now her eyes swell. "You were making bombs?"

"Not the bombs," I tell her softly. "The balloons that will carry the bombs on the wind."

"Balloons?" She looks like she wants to put her hand to my forehead to feel for fever.

"Huge balloons, Auntie. And huge bombs. Exploding and burning all across America."

Now she joins me at the table. I see one of the worry lines on her face relax, then tighten again. "Sending off balloons willy-nilly. It's like grasping clouds."

"No, Auntie. It will work. I haven't explained it well enough, that's all."

"Let me get you something to eat." She gets up from her cushion.

"Wait, have your heard anything about Suki?" I ask. "She got ill. Is she . . . ?"

Auntie touches my shoulder. "Suki is resting at home. She's still very sick—no visitors allowed—but she's getting better."

I want to cry with joy, but I'm too tired for that, too. Instead, I eat a little gray rice and crawl onto my futon, still hungry and bone-tired, but very glad to be back.

That's where I am now, lying on my back in the room I share with my aunt, watching the dusk turn to darkness. For the first time since I left for Kure City all those weeks ago, I feel my ancestors around me. They sit at my side, but they don't speak. They want me to sleep. Tomorrow I'll have to start worrying again—about Kyo, about Suki, about the hunger gnawing at my belly. But tomorrow is not for many hours. There's no rush—our woes are patient houseguests, watchful all night and still here in the morning.

This is the first time I'm leaving the cottage since I returned home three days ago. We're almost out of food, so I must get some, and that's not easy. There's nothing at the stores, and Auntie has heard that Pāru has no food left to trade. My kumquat-size belly turns inside out in panic, until I remember something. I recall Grandmother saying her family ate acorns during hungry times. I ask Auntie if she knows how to prepare them, and she does. She will teach me . . . if I can find any.

At the village park, I manage to fill a small sack with nuts from the old oak tree. The first thing my aunt does when I hand them over is dump them into a pot of cold water out front.

"Toss out the ones that float," she instructs.

"Why?"

"Worms. Or beetles."

"Oh." I'm sorry I asked.

"Let the rest soak. It will soften the shells."

A couple of hours later, I take a nutcracker onto the front step and start shelling. "Can I eat a few while I work?" I ask.

"Only if you want to spend the rest of the day throwing up," Auntie warns. "We have to soak out the poison first."

"How long will that take?"

"A few hours."

I feel my face fall. Time moves so slowly when you're hungry. A few hours isn't just the rest of the morning—it's enough time for an acorn to grow into a giant oak.

"Go take a rest, Tamiko," she says. "It will help pass the time."

Lying here on my futon, I try to fill the hours with remembering. I remember how Kyo and I used to gorge ourselves on Grandmother's scattered sushi. I remember last summer at the farm when we ate sweet egg tamagoyaki almost every morning. I conjure up the tang of fresh persimmons and apples. On and on I remember. I have nothing else to do with myself, after all: no thread, no school, and Suki is still sick. So I dream of days gone by.

And of days to come. When Kyo returns and Suki is well. When we have fish and white rice and noodles on our table. When we greet each new morning without fear. When the ten thousand balloons have done their work and there is peace. A universal brotherhood for our Emperor.

Today, Auntie sends me to Pāru with a small glass picture frame to trade, hoping Pāru might have scrounged up a few beans or a rice cake by now. When I get there, she's sitting on her front step, head down, eyes on the straw sandals that sit next to her bare feet. Her toes must be cold in this early spring air.

"Ohayō!" I call out good morning to get her attention.

Pāru looks up. "Tamiko, I haven't seen you in a long while. Come, sit." She pats a spot on the step next to her.

I obey.

"Have you brought me some good news?" she asks.

"I've brought you a lovely frame." I pull it from my pocket and hold it out to her.

She looks but doesn't pick it up. Then she returns her gaze to her sandals. My heart sinks.

"This frame is one of my aunt's prized belongings," I offer. "Look, do you see the blossoms cut into the glass?"

"Yes, it's a fine specimen." She twines her fingers, exposing the split and yellowed nails. "But I have nothing left to trade for it." Her voice is papery and a little unsteady. "Nothing left at all."

Poor Pāru. She's as hungry as I am, and she's all alone.

I don't know how to be with her, how to comfort her. Grandmother said that not-speaking is the flower. But she also said that one kind word can warm three snowy peaks. I try for the kind word, but I can't think of one that's also true, so I say nothing.

We simply sit, Pāru digging her toes into the dirt, me racking my brain, the sun climbing toward noon. The day is so quiet, I think I actually hear Pāru's heart fracture. It frightens me. I stand up.

"Sayounara, Tamiko," she says. Not *jaa ne* or *mata ne* or any of the other ways to say see you. Sayounara. Farewell. It sounds final.

I reach my hand to her. "Please, Pāru, come home with me. Auntie has a pot of acorns on the boil."

Her cloudy eyes fill with surprise, as if no one has ever given her anything, as if everything is a trade, a deal. "But I don't have enough teeth. Not in back, where it counts."

"No matter. We can grind the nuts. You'll see."

She looks lost. "What will your aunt say, another mouth to feed?"

"She'll say, 'How nice to see you, Pāru-san.'" I bring my hand closer to hers, and she finally takes it.

I can't say the acorns are delicious, but they busy our mouths and fill our bellies. Pāru and Auntie gab like old friends. They reminisce and gossip and predict. Sitting here with these two old ladies, I can almost imagine a proper lunch, one with real food and a lazy afternoon ahead of us. I can nearly picture it.

21
NELLIE
May 5, 1945

Picnic day! It's a few minutes after noon when the pastor pulls up in his white Chevrolet. Well, not really white anymore. Not like the shooting star—if that's what it was—that zigzagged overhead last night. More like the twins' socks. I'm the last pickup, so I end up sitting on Joan Patzke's lap up front next to Mrs. Mitchell. Joey is squashed in back with Eddie Engen, Jay Gifford, Sherman Shoemaker, and Joan's brother, Dick. A full load.

"No fishing pole?" asks the pastor. "I have an extra in the trunk, if you don't mind sharing it with Sherman." That's the pastor for you, always watching out for everyone. He's going to be a great father when his baby comes along.

"I'm not really much for fishing," I tell him.

"You and me both." He winks.

We head out. Pretty soon we're driving through town, past the post office, past the Antler Grill, the filling station, and the novelty shop the twins adore. Then we turn onto the logging road. It's a postcard kind of day, the sky clear and the air dry after last night's rain, a fine day for a picnic.

Joey sits directly behind me, which makes me wish I'd spent more time brushing my mop in the back this morning. Oh, well. At twelve thirty sharp, Mrs. Mitchell turns on the radio so we can hear the headlines as we sail along. "Formal negotiations for Germany's full surrender began today in the city of Reims, France." We all cheer. "The Allied Forces have all but secured Burma." More whistles and whoops. "The Allies continue their assault on Okinawa." We applaud. Final victory feels as close as the next mailbox on the road up ahead.

It's another ten miles to Gearhart Mountain. We're in such high spirits, we don't even notice the pastor slowing way down, not until he comes to a full stop right in the middle of the logging road. In front of us stands a sawhorse with a sign saying ROAD CLOSED FOR GRADING. The car fills with groans so loud, you'd think the sign means HITLER STILL ALIVE instead of PICNIC ABORTED.

"Let's go to Leonard Creek instead," I say. "I used to hike there with my pa. People were always pulling heaps of trout out."

Just like that, the pastor makes a U-turn and Gearhart Mountain rises purple and snow-capped behind us. If last night's falling star, or whatever it was, landed on the mountain, I'll never know.

It's a short drive to the turnoff for the creek. Soon we're cruising up the muddy road past the pine stands and rock flats of Fremont National Forest. Before us, the hills are flush with juniper trees, and the aspens quake in the breeze. Then the creek comes into view, rippling over the stony bottom in its race toward lower ground.

"Oh, Archie, this looks like the perfect spot," says Mrs. Mitchell, her hand on her belly. She's right—there's a thicket of trees, but not too thick, and then a small field leading down to the water.

"Yes, all right, Elsye dear." He pulls over. "I'll have to find a clearing for the car, but I'll drop you off here. Boys, you carry the picnic basket for Mrs. Mitchell." We all start to hop out when he adds, "Joey, why don't you ride along with me?"

What's that about? I hope they won't be gone long—the day is already flying by.

We take the basket, blanket, and fishing poles out of the trunk. By the time the white Chevrolet takes the first bend in the road, we're halfway to the creek. Sherman, who's the youngest, peels off to start exploring the woods. The rest of us spread out the blanket and set down the basket and poles.

"This will do nicely." Mrs. Mitchell surveys our camp. "We'll have lunch as soon as the pastor and Joey get here." She's eating for two now, so she's probably extra hungry.

The boys start digging for bait worms, and Joan slices the pie, and I take off my shoes and head down to the creek. Dipping my toes in the icy water, I try to imagine summer. Maybe the war will be over by then. Maybe we'll wipe out the Japanese and Pa will be home come June or July. Maybe by the time this stream is warm enough to wade in, everything will be like it used to be, like it should be.

Except that things will never be like they used to be for Joey.

I hope he doesn't hate me for that, for having Pa back. I hope we'll be best friends again by then. I hope today marks a new start for us.

I pull my foot out of the water, so cold it burns. This stream has a whole lot of warming up to do before anyone can go in past their ankles, but that's okay. I can still feel summer coming.

Joan appears at my side, shading her eyes with her hand. "How's the water?"

"Perfect."

She looks the creek up and down. "I've never gone fishing before."

"You're not missing much."

"Really? Dick always makes it sound like oodles of fun."

"My brothers do too. It's a bore if you ask me. You finish the math homework yet?"

"Haven't started it."

"Me either," I say. "Hey, you still have that scraggly kitten you found under your father's truck?"

"Not a kitten anymore. She's big as a barn cat now. You still have your dog—What's her name? Pip?"

"Kip. That's my Uncle Clem's dog. He brings her when he's down from Klamath Falls."

Then we hear Mrs. Mitchell calling out. "I'm going to see where Sherman ran off to. Anyone want to join me?"

"I will, Mrs. Mitchell," Joan calls back.

"Me too," say the boys.

"Are you coming?" Joan asks.

"I have to get my shoes," I say. "Go on along, and I'll catch up."

With Joan in the lead, they all head toward the trees. I take my time walking back to my loafers. Sitting down on the blanket and pulling my socks back on, my mind turns to Joey and the pastor. What's taking them so long? It couldn't be that hard to find a spot for the car. Maybe Pastor Mitchell wants to talk to Joey about something. I want to talk to Joey too—about anything, really.

As I stand up to step into my shoes, I hear Joan's voice through the trees. "Hey, Nellie, come look what we found."

A rabbit nest, I figure, or maybe a foxhole. I'll join them in a minute, but I like being here alone, just me and the creek and the promise of summer on its way. Plus, Joey might arrive any second . . .

"Nellie, c'mon!" Joan calls again. "You have to see this."

"Coming."

I turn in the direction of Joan's voice, but before I take more than a few steps, there's an incredible sound, a roar. Like fireworks, except there are no fireworks in the middle of a forest. Like the loudest peal of thunder, except there's no storm. Like cannons, except there's no battlefield here. None of those things is here. There are only huge branches hurtling above the trees in a dusty, smoky burst, and hundreds and hundreds of twigs filling up the air.

What do I do? Run into that? Run away? I can't hear Joan anymore. Where is she? Where's the pastor? My legs are about to give way. Where's Joey?

22

TAMIKO

February 23, 1945

Suki's mother finally gave me permission to visit today—how happy I'll be to see my friend! I've missed her so much, and I want her to know—to know I've thought about her, worried about her, every day, every hour. It's a long walk to her house on the other side of town, but it doesn't matter. Seeing Suki is what matters.

Before I'm allowed to be in the same room with her, her sister, Fuyumi, points me to the kitchen and makes me wash my hands—twice. Her little brother, Nori, thinks this is very funny. It's good to hear laughter again, especially the giggles little boys make.

In the next room, Suki is draped across the futon, looking much better than the day she left the washi factory. She was so colorless then, I could almost see right through her, like a glass of water. Now she's solid again. Not that she looks hearty. No, she's still frail, but she's recovering, thanks to her mother's good care and her sister's watchfulness.

"Suki!" I cry out and rush over to her.

"Tamiko, at last." She pulls in her knees to make room for me on the futon, and we hug.

"You look well, my friend."

"No, not well. But better, better than I was."

Now that I'm sitting next to her, I see the shadows under her eyes, the flatness of her hair, how she has bitten her nails down to the quick. But she's improving, and that's what counts. Even if her voice is still weary and her skin drained, she's getting better.

"Tell me everything," she says. "I feel galaxies away with this quarantine. Tell me everything you know."

"Have you been listening to the radio?"

"The radio is my only companion these days."

"So you know about our balloon bombs?" I ask.

"Many fires in America. Many deaths, much terror, great revenge."

"Ten thousand revenges," I beam. "And we had a hand in it."

She coughs, but it's not the wild, barking cough she had in Kure.

"Our handsome soldier praised you," I add. "He said you served our Emperor well."

A drop of color dots her face. "I don't deserve praise for what I did."

"You only left a few days early. You get as much glory as the rest of us."

She shakes her head. "I'm not sure any of us deserves glory." Her tone is pinched. "What we did is killing, Tamiko. Killing innocent people by our own hands."

The hair on the back of my neck stands up like soldiers at attention. "But defeating the Americans is part of the divine plan, Suki."

"I know." She slumps back against the futon. "That's what makes it so hard. I don't know how to feel."

That's because she doesn't have a brother in the fight.

She's right here with her whole family. They'll be together no matter how long the war lasts, no matter how many battles.

"Well, I know how you should feel." I touch her arm. "Happy. Proud."

"Do you really think so? Because—"

"I know so," I interrupt. "The sooner we cripple the Americans, the sooner we win the war."

She still looks troubled.

"And the sooner we win, the sooner things get better," I go on. "The sooner we eat. The sooner our soldiers come home. The sooner the divine plan comes true."

"Yes," Suki says. But she doesn't sound convinced. She rearranges herself on the futon. "Do you have any gossip? I haven't had a decent piece of chitchat in ages."

So she wants to change the subject. All right. I scoot closer and start to braid her hair. "I heard Eguchi-sensei married our assistant teacher."

"What?" she says. "Eguchi-sensei and little Terada-sensei? But she's so young and he's so . . ."

"Not that old, not really. He just acts that way."

"I suppose. What a time to get married, though. Surely, there was no white kimono, no special meal, no gifts."

"No," I say, working her hair, "but this is no time to live alone, either."

"Like your poor aunt while you were away. How is she?"

"She's all right. Worried for Kyo."

"No word from him?"

"No."

"I'm sorry, Tamiko."

I shrug. "If it's true that bad news has wings, then he must be safe and sound."

Suki nods.

"Is Fuyumi still planning to go to work in the steel factory?" I ask.

"Not if my mother gets her way."

"Your mother always gets her way." I finish the braid.

"Mm . . . are you hungry?"

Of course I'm hungry. Everyone is hungry. But no one has anything to spare. "I'm fine."

Suki doesn't believe me, and there's a clumsy silence.

That's when I notice the book on the floor by her side. I pick up a short story collection. "I'll read to you, how's that? Like you did for me last year when I sprained my ankle."

"All right, but I warn you, those stories are eerie. Fuyumi lent them to me."

I find where Suki left off and begin reading "The Human Chair" by Edogawa Ranpo. "Yoshiko saw her husband off to his work at the Foreign Office at a little past ten o'clock," I begin. Suki curls herself up a little tighter and settles in.

Eerie is right. The story is about a craftsman who builds a

large armchair for a hotel lobby, and then decides to hide himself in the space under the cushions. Every day he eavesdrops on the people who sit on the chair. Every night he sneaks out to rob the guest rooms. Except, that isn't really what happens in the story. The author is tricking us. It's strange. And distracting—which is exactly what we need.

By the time I finish the tale, Suki is all but asleep, nestled next to me on the futon. It reminds me of the way we huddled together on our cotton mats under our thin blankets in Kure. There's so much more to talk about, to remember, to plan. But it will have to wait.

I put the book back on the floor and tiptoe out of the room. When she wakes up, I hope she sees I'm right about the balloon bombs. I hope she can take pride in her honorable work. She deserves that.

23
NELLIE
May 5, 1945

Joey and the pastor went to get some help. I'm here alone up on Leonard Creek. Alone with the smoky black and nightmare red and dirty white. All the others are gone: Mrs. Mitchell, Joan, Dick, Eddie, Jay, and Sherman.

It's quiet, ear-splittingly quiet. I want to scream. I can't. It's too late for prayers, but still, I pray every prayer I can think of.

Can God even hear them?

Is God even real?

The only thing that's real is what I saw. Fire. Smoke. Trees hurtling into space, branches whirling. Dead bodies. And . . . the enormous deflated balloon lying to the side, partly covered by a snowdrift. The thing that blew up and killed them. Mrs. Mitchell, Joan, Dick, Eddie, Jay, and Sherman.

Here's what I do while I wait: I remember everything I can. Sherman won the soapbox derby last year. He made his racecar out of, I don't know, an old table from his backyard, I think. It was blue, he painted it blue. Jay, he fell out of a tree and broke his arm in fourth grade. He cried, and we made fun of him.

Joan Patzke could eat more hot dogs than anyone I know. And . . . she had bad breath . . . It's true, that's what I remember about her. That's all I can remember about her.

Dick and Eddie, they played the donkey in the church Christmas play one year. I can't remember who was the head and who was the tail, but one of them stopped while the other one kept walking. Ripped the donkey costume clear in half. Poor Mrs. Mitchell, she'd worked hard on that costume.

Poor Mrs. Mitchell.

I feel dizzy. Blood crashing against my temples. Lungs refusing to fill. I wish Pa were standing here next to me. I'd do anything to have him with me right now.

Here are the things I don't do while I wait. I don't breathe through my nose. I don't rub my eyes. I don't face the hole in the ground.

Time decides to play a crazy trick on me, and I see it all over again, right in front of me. Flames lick Mrs. Mitchell's shoes. Smoke rises from Sherman's hair, like it's carrying a message somewhere. And above it all, pine needles fall dreamy as snow, dusting all of them, covering them, burying them.

All on account of that white balloon, bigger than life. What on earth? A balloon.

"Miss?" a voice is suddenly behind me.

"Hmm, what?" I turn to see two men in ranger uniforms alongside Joey and the pastor. Pastor Mitchell's normally slicked-back hair is hanging into his eyes like a horse's forelock. Tears have cut a path down his flushed cheeks. Joey is wild-eyed and as white as a shooting star. I think they're both in shock.

"I said, are you all right, miss?" the older ranger asks.

"Uh . . ."

The younger ranger walks on to the hole. He's carrying a pile of sheets, blankets, and first-aid supplies. Why? It's no use now—doesn't he see that? Didn't the pastor tell him what happened?

The older ranger takes the pastor aside and starts asking him a thousand questions. Then he starts in with Joey. The younger ranger comes to quiz me.

"Hello," he says, tossing his bundle onto the ground. "I'm Ranger Baranski."

"Hullo," I manage.

"You probably don't feel much like talking, but I do need to ask you a few things." He pulls a small notebook from his pocket and blinks his gray eyes. "Maybe you can start with your name and address."

"I'm Nellie Doud. Forty-two Danby Road in Bly."

He nods and jots his note. Mournful. Sad. All I feel is smoke in my nose and a horrible roar in my ears.

"Now Nellie, I understand you were the first one on the scene." He pushes his ranger hat a little higher on his head. "Can you tell me everything you remember, everything you saw and heard?"

I clutch my belly like the insides are going to fall out of me. I never knew what a single bomb could do. How much ruin. How much loss. "Well, Sherman, he's the youngest, he went into the woods as soon as we got to the creek. Then Mrs. Mitchell and the others went to find him."

"Uh-huh."

I tell him how Joan called for me to come see what they found. How I didn't get a chance on account of the explosion. And then I start to tear up.

"I'm sorry." The ranger puts his hand on my shoulder. "I'm sorry you had to . . . go through this. Take your time now."

"All I could see at first were branches flying and—and smoke. I ran closer, and that's when I saw the fire."

My fingers start to tingle as I talk.

Was it just two hours ago I was sitting on a bony lap next to a woman with a baby growing in her?

"Then Joey and the pastor came running over," I tell him. "We cleared some of the branches. The pastor tried to put out the fire on Mrs. Mitchell's dress. We checked to see if anyone was . . . y'know . . . breathing." I sniff back the image. "Then the pastor and Joey went to find you."

"And this thing." The ranger points to the balloon. "Was it here the whole time—or did you see it fall from the sky?"

"Um . . ." I can't think.

"It must've already been here," the ranger says. "Explains the reports of falling stars last night."

Falling stars.

Is this my falling star?

Is this my wish-making, good-fortune-bringing orb, the thing I imagined twinkling in the brush atop Gearhart Mountain?

I feel a scream hardening in my gut, a terrible howl moving into my lungs and up to my throat. But when it reaches my lips, it's nothing but a muffled word. "No," I mumble. "Please, no."

The ranger thinks I'm talking to him. "All right, we can stop. This has been very helpful." He shoves his notebook back in his pocket. "Come along now, Nellie. We'll take you and your friends back to your car." He turns to the others. "Ready to go, you two?"

Pastor Mitchell doesn't seem to hear him. "May I use your telephone?" he asks. "I need to make arrangements for my wife and these children to be brought back to Bly."

"I'm afraid that's not possible," says the older ranger. "Nothing can be removed until the navy people get here from Whidbey Island. That will be hours. Nightfall."

Navy people. Navy people?

"But I mustn't leave them," the pastor pleads. "I can't leave my wife, my . . ."

"I'm afraid you must." The ranger takes the pastor's arm and leads him away.

We reach the Chevy, and the pastor stands there for a moment, confused, like he doesn't know his own car. Or maybe he doesn't understand why it's empty, why Mrs. Mitchell isn't sitting there, hand on her belly, smiling because we've found the perfect spot for a picnic. When the ranger finally opens the passenger door, the pastor slides in, all glassy-eyed and wet-cheeked, right where his wife is supposed to be. It's the lonesomest sight I've ever seen.

The ride home is awful. Joey drives—he gets behind the wheel without even asking—and I sit in the back alone, staring out the window. I wish someone would say something. The quiet is so miserably loud. But if I speak, I'll say the wrong thing, so I don't. *Hurry up, Joey, get us out of here.*

Joey pulls up in front of my house. I start to get out when the pastor says shakily, "I want to tell your mother what happened. Yours too, Joey."

Joey and I glance at each other. The pastor doesn't look well enough for this terrible errand. His face is chalk, his eyes shot through with red. He's smaller than he was this morning, his body shrunken inside his jacket, like half the life got sucked out of him. He opens the door but can barely swing his leg out.

"I'll get you inside," Joey says. He comes around and helps the pastor out of the car. I take the pastor's other arm, and we head up my driveway into the house.

When the screen door slaps shut behind us, Mother calls from the kitchen, "You home already?" Then she appears in the doorway, sees that I'm not alone, and takes one look at our faces. "Dear heaven, what happened?"

Suddenly I have to get some fresh air. I can't help it. The pastor shouldn't have to do this alone, but I think I'm going to burst if I don't get outside. "I'll be . . ." I say, pointing to the outdoors. "I'm going—"

Mother takes the pastor from us. "You stay right here, young lady."

"Can't." I run out to the front steps and drop against the railing.

Joey joins me. He stands by the opposite railing, his back to me. We stay there like that, statues, until he finally breaks the hush. "We left all the picnic stuff there," he says in a far-off voice.

"Oh, yeah."

"Lucky for the squirrels."

"Mm." I knead my hands, my legs.

"Damn those road graders."

"What?"

"The roadblock." He practically spits the words. "It's the only reason we ended up at Leonard Creek in the first place."

"No, *I'm* the only reason we ended up at Leonard Creek. I'm the one who said let's go there, remember?"

He turns around to face me. "Nell, I didn't mean—"

"It's okay, forget about it. Hey, what were you two talking about when you went to park the car? Did he want you to start coming back to church?"

"No. I mean, sure, he wants that, but it's not what we talked about." He shifts his weight from one foot to the other, like he's trying to get away from my question. "He was asking how I'm doing. You know, how I'm doing since . . ." He clears his throat. "Since my brother. Sorry, I still can't say his name. Haven't said it since he died—since he got killed."

"I'm sorry, Joey. I don't think I ever said so. I'm sorry about your brother. About Peter."

"That's what the pastor said too. To start with. Then he said some other stuff I didn't like." He swallows hard. "Stuff about accepting it. Made me steam right up. Did you hear me yelling at him?"

I shake my head.

"Well, we'll see how the pastor feels about accepting things now." He puts a fist on the railing. "We'll just see how he feels."

I can't take my eyes off Joey's balled-up hand. "Did you see the look on the pastor when we first uncovered Mrs. Mitchell?" I ask. "I hardly recognized him."

"Yeah . . . Say, did you see it happen, Nell? See the bomb go off?"

"No."

His forehead wrinkles like he's worried.

"What?"

"I dunno," he says. "I just think you'd be better off if you did see it."

"Better off? Then I'd see it every time I close my eyes."

"Yup. But that's all you'd see. It would be easier."

"What are you talking about, Joey?"

"Lookit." He sticks his hands in his pockets. "When my brother got killed, I didn't see that happen either. I don't know if he died instantly, or if he agonized, or if he had a buddy with him, or anything. When I close my eyes? I see it happening every possible way. All the hundreds and thousands of ways the Nazis can kill an American soldier, that's what I see every single night."

A wild current pulses through my belly. "I bet that makes you mad."

"Furious."

"Maybe even mad enough to start a fire in someone's shed."

Joey's cheeks go scarlet. His eyes fill with something, I don't know what—fear, maybe, or more hate.

"I threw my spyglass to warn you Mr. Kava was coming," I finally admit. "'Cause you were kind of hypnotized by the fire."

Joey's face goes blank for a second, and then he blinks. "So *that's* what that banging sound was. I—"

Suddenly Mother is here, wrapping her arms around me and

clutching me tight. The pastor is behind her, and the twins are inside with their noses pressed against the screen.

"Nellie," she chokes. "My dear Nellie."

I don't know what to do. Mother hasn't hugged me in ages. Now she's holding on to me like I'm the most precious thing in her world. "I'm here," I say gingerly. "I'm here."

Then I melt into her and press my face against her shoulder, breathing in the smells of coffee and soap, cooking and gardening, the smells of normal. I don't want it to end.

She leans back and examines my face and arms for, I don't know, cuts or burns, I guess. "Are you all right?"

I nod, holding back my tears. "I was over by the creek when it happened."

"Thank the Lord." She clasps me again, rocking back and forth. "Let's get you inside. I'll fix you something to drink, and you'll tell me everything. Come on."

"But . . ." I don't want to go inside, not yet. I'm not ready to face Mother's questions, not sure I want to retell the story again.

"I hope you can get some rest tonight, Nellie," the pastor says. "I hope . . ." His voice trails off.

"I'll just help them get across the street," I tell Mother. "I'll be right back, I promise."

She's about to say no, I can see it, but then she stops herself. "Right back, you hear?"

I take the pastor's arm. "I hear."

The three of us trudge across the street, and as we go, I notice something strange, something unexpected about the pastor. He doesn't look angry. Not at the unknown bomber. Not at Sherman for dilly-dallying in the woods and forcing Mrs. Mitchell to go looking for him. Not at Joan Patzke or whoever discovered the balloon. Not at God for making a world where terrible things can happen. No one. There's no hate in his eyes, no fury.

Oh, his hair is still a mess, and his shoulders are still wilted, but he looks . . . I don't know . . . steady, calm. Not like he's past this disaster—I don't think he'll ever be past it—but above it, beyond it. I can't imagine how.

We make it up the driveway onto the Coopers' porch. As Joey steps into his house with the pastor, he mouths to me, "Hold up a second."

Before I have a chance to say anything, he disappears inside, so I have no choice but to wait. Through the screen door, I hear the pastor greet Mrs. Cooper while Poppy offers a lazy woof, and then Joey is back.

"Nellie, look," he starts.

"I'm sorry, Joey. I wasn't gonna say anything about the shed. I never should've, today of all days. I'm just crazy today. But you don't have to worry. I—"

"Nellie," he says, but a little softer this time. "I want to say thank you, that's all."

"Uh . . . oh."

"I've been wondering what that noise was." He rubs his chin. "I don't know how you knew, how you ended up there, but, yeah, you saved my hide."

"Maybe. Or maybe Mr. Kava would've understood in the end."

"Not a chance."

"I won't tell anyone, I promise."

"I know." He looks down at his feet. "And listen, that stuff I said about seeing things when you close your eyes? Forget it. That's me, not you. You'll do better than that, you'll see."

"How do you know?" I ask.

"I just know."

I start to wave his words away, but he catches my hand in his.

"I know it because you're better than me," he says. "You always have been."

Suddenly I'm not sure I can stay upright. I'm dizzy all over again, and my legs are jelly.

"Nellie, you okay?" I vaguely hear him ask. He's still holding my hand, and now his other hand is on my shoulder.

"I'm fine. I . . . you know." I let go of his hand and run home. It's all I can do.

In the kitchen, Willie and Henry are wide-eyed and dumb-struck, like they're looking at a ghost. They watch Mother lead me to the table and help me into a chair. It doesn't take long for them to find their voices, though.

"Did they really blow up?" Henry plunks into the seat next to me.

"What did the bomb look like?" Willie pipes up.

"That's enough, boys." Mother sets a glass of milk in front of me. "Drink this up now, Nellie."

My stomach turns. "I can't."

"Just a couple of sips?" Mother tries.

I shake my head.

"Was it loud?" Willie asks. "Tell us everything."

"Yeah, tell us," Henry coaxes. "Did it make you want to upchuck?"

"Will you both SHUT UP?" I yell.

I jump out of the chair and run upstairs, slamming my bedroom door behind me. The first thing I do is shove everything off my nightstand—alarm clock, books, magazines, sending them clanking onto the wood floor. Then I throw my covers off the bed, howling some throaty sound I've never made before. I'm sure they hear me downstairs, but no one comes near me, and it's a good thing. I hate them all right now, every one of them. I flop onto my bare bed.

When Mother checks on me later, I pretend to be asleep. I do try to sleep, try to fall into a dream—maybe a half dream, even a quarter dream, but nothing. My mind won't quit. Joey was right—I don't see the bomb when I close my eyes. But I do hear it. So loud, so heavy, like a thousand trees falling at once. Ten thousand trees.

Around midnight, I lift my blackout shade and open my window. I look across the street to the Coopers' house and beyond to Gearhart Mountain and finally up to the universe that twinkles down at me. I know I'll never understand this world, this day, half as well as I do these skies. I wonder if Pa is looking up at the sky right now too. I say a little prayer that he comes home soon. Then I crawl back to bed and wait for this sleepless night to pass.

24

TAMIKO

March 12, 1945

The Americans have bombed Tokyo. We didn't get the news for a full day after it happened, but now we're bombarded with stories about fire raining down on our Emperor's capital. They say you can see the blaze as far away as Mount Fuji. They say the smoke is vaster and deadlier than a thousand angry dragons. There's no way to know which stories are true, but this we do know: It was terrible.

That's why they've dug holes behind our school, like makeshift shelters. And it's why the small children have been evacuated from Shinji-cho, all of them swept away to inns, temples, and homes in the countryside, where we suppose they will be safer. Even Suki's little brother Nori, barely five years old, has been sent away. It's so quiet here now, you could hear a blossom petal fall—or a needle or a strand of thread.

Eguchi-sensei,

We haven't had school in a long time, but I remember how you taught us the Emperor's words. You taught us that we're a hundred million hearts beating as one. We must all fight together for Japan's victory. Everything is so different now. Now our Emperor tells us we're a hundred million shattered jewels, that we should all die together rather than surrender. I'm ready for that, ready to fight to the death, if I only knew how. Kyo is ready to fight to the death too, and he may already have done so, which is the saddest part, for he's the brightest jewel of them all.

Eguchi-sensei, is victory truly beyond our grasp? I still want to believe that our soldiers and our balloon bombs and our divine purpose can defeat the enemy. Do you believe?

I'll pray for my brother. I'll pray for you and your bride. And I'll pray for the strength to fight, even if my only weapon is a prayer.

~ Tamiko

"The place where Nori is staying, I hope they're good to him," Suki says when I visit today. We sit on the futon, our feet tucked under us.

"I'm sure they're being kind," I offer.

"I hope there's another little boy there for him to play with." She twirls her pigtail around her finger. "And enough rice."

"No one would take him in if they couldn't feed him."

"Well, we'll visit him sometime soon, and then we'll see for ourselves."

"Good." I fold my arms. "And curse those Americans for making him have to leave."

"Can you blame them?"

"Who?" I ask.

"The Americans." She uncoils her legs. "They're only taking revenge on our revenge. On our balloon bombs."

I half laugh, then stiffen. Suki is my best friend. I thought I knew her completely. But lately I don't even know whose side she's on. "Are you really blaming our balloons for what the enemy did to our Emperor's city?"

Suki lets out a breath. "What I'm saying, Tamiko, is that the balloon bombs were supposed to end the war. But that didn't happen. Instead, they made it worse."

"No!" I protest. "The balloons didn't make it worse. The Americans made it worse. Worse for you, worse for Nori, worse for Kyo."

"You know"—she rubs her forehead—"if we didn't send the balloons, Nori and Kyo might be home by now."

"Don't say that!" Hot tears spring to my eyes. "Don't say it's my fault they're away."

"Not your fault alone. Mine, too." Then she says it again more gently. "Mine, too."

I push myself away from her until I'm tottering at the edge of the futon. "You make me sound like a criminal, like I'm trying to keep Kyo away at war. Listen to me, Suki. The only reason I went to Kure City in the first place was to help get him back."

"You meant well." She nods. "So did I. But we were wrong. All that konnyaku root gone to waste. Gone to America, when it could have fed us."

"It is not a waste. It's so the Emperor can unite the world. 'Eight corners of the world under one roof,' remember?"

"I think there's more than one way to bring the world together," Suki says. "Aren't you hungry, Tamiko?"

Blood pounds in my temples.

"I'm hungry, all the time," she admits. "I can't sleep at night because my belly growls so loud. My conscience growls even louder."

I jump up from the futon. I can't listen to another word. "You know what? I have to go. Say hello to Nori for me when you visit."

I hurry out of the house so no one will see me crying. Now I face the long walk home. The sky is grayer than konnyaku paste this afternoon, as gray as ashes. I can't believe the things Suki said. She's wrong. Wrong to pick a fight with me, wrong to think the way she does.

Still, I can't believe I quarreled with her. She's frail and frightened. She's my best friend. Who will I talk to now? How will I get through this war without her?

25

NELLIE

May 6, 1945

"What are you doing up?" Mother asks when she finds me in the kitchen, slicing bread at the counter. "I told you there wouldn't be school today."

"Couldn't sleep."

"Maybe I shouldn't go to work. You don't look well." She's not affectionate like she was yesterday. She's more like her old self, except that her hair looks a little grayer, the lines around her eyes a little deeper. Worry lines.

"I'm fine, Mother," I say. "Coffee's on."

"You could have woken me, you know."

"Hmm?"

"When you couldn't sleep. You could have gotten me. I probably wasn't asleep anyway."

"Oh. Yeah." I shove two pieces of bread into the toaster and bring the butter dish to the table, almost tripping on the braided rug as I do.

"What will you do with yourself all day?" she asks.

"I'm sure the twins will keep me busy. They want to walk into town. Maybe we'll do that."

"Ruby too?"

"Probably," I say.

"Good."

"Why?"

"You should have someone with you today." She sits down and plays with the corner of the cookbook that's still lying open on the table. "Someone you can talk to. You'll want that, you'll see."

"I'm done talking," I say, more sharply than I mean to.

Mother raises an eyebrow, takes a sip of her coffee. "You know, I bet this same conversation is happening across the street right now."

No, Joey's probably smart enough to stay in bed.

"Thank heavens Joey didn't get caught in the blast," Mother says. "Can you imagine if they lost both their sons? If I were Mrs. Cooper, I'd keep that boy on a leash."

I let out a small laugh.

"What?" she says.

"I guess I'm more dispensable than Joey, seeing how you have the twins as backup children."

"Nellie! You know I didn't mean it like that."

"Well, it sure sounded like it." The toast pops, but I let it sit.

"You're every bit as important to me as Joey is to them."

I roll my eyes. "You hug me exactly once since Pa's been away, and all of a sudden I'm supposed to believe I'm important to you?"

Her mouth unlatches.

"Never mind," I tell her. "I'm getting dressed."

"I'll try to stop home at lunchtime," I hear her say when I'm already on the stairs.

"We'll probably be out," I call down, because it's easier than saying sorry. Then I shove my bedroom door shut so she won't hear me sob.

As the twins and I walk up the road to Ruby's, I'm thinking she might still be sleeping, but she's not. She's in the aviary, feeding the doves.

"Nellie, Nellie, Nellie!" She shouts when she spots us coming. She races over and throws her arms around me, squeezing so tight I can hardly breathe. "Gramps and I were up at Aunt Wendy's over in Beatty. I didn't hear till we got home, and Gramps wouldn't let me come over, said it was too late. I couldn't sleep all night. Are you all right?"

"Yeah, I guess so."

"You have to tell me everything." She steps back and turns to the boys. "Willie and Henry, you go to the aviary. Nellie and I have to talk."

The boys run off, shouting to the birds, telling each other the last one there is a rotten pigeon egg.

"Every detail." Ruby takes my arm and leads me to the front steps. "Tell me everything. Don't leave a single thing out."

All at once, I realize Mother was right—I do need someone to talk to. Someone I can tell the whole story to, someone who really knows me. We sit on the steps, and I try to find somewhere to begin. I tell Ruby how happy and noisy we all were on the ride out, with me on Joan's bony lap and the five boys squashed into the back. How beautiful it was up there, the creek like a taste of summer. I tell her about the blast, the terrible loudness of it. The flying branches, the reeking smoke.

"Rubes . . . Mrs. Mitchell's dress was on fire. The pastor tried to put it out with his bare hands. He fell on the ground and wept and cursed and pounded his fist. It was awful."

Ruby squeezes my wrist.

"And when our eyes met—oh, Rubes—I think the pastor was afraid of me. Like, maybe I'm not real. Maybe I'm a ghost. Or maybe he's making me up."

Ruby gets teary, and we just sit there for a while. Then she takes a breath and lets go of my wrist. "Did you hear what they're saying, Nell? What they're thinking it is?"

I wipe my eyes on my sleeve. "What—who?"

"Listen," she scooches closer. "Gramps was talking to his friends over at the VFW. And they said . . ." She looks over her shoulder to make sure the twins aren't nearby. "They said the bomb was an enemy attack."

"An enemy"—a jolt of electricity runs through my chest—"attack?"

"That's why the navy men got called in," she says. "They don't know who it was yet, but they'll find out, all right."

I drop my forehead onto my knees.

Ruby makes a clicking noise out of the side of her mouth. "Wonder if it was Japan or Germany. Probably Japan, I'll betcha."

"Or maybe . . ." I think about what Irene Kava said in the schoolyard the other day, about the Japanese people coming home from the camps, about how maybe they want revenge. And why shouldn't they be resentful? We caged them up even though they're Americans, even though they have nothing to do with the enemy. I know I'd be bitter. Bitter and maybe vengeful, too. Then I force the thought out.

"What's that, Nellie Bly?" she asks.

"Hmm? Oh, nothing." I push myself up off the steps. "Hey, I'm gonna buy some flour and butter and make something nice for the pastor. Wanna come?"

She squints up at me. "It won't make him feel any better, y'know."

"I know, but it's all I can think to do." And I need to do something.

The muddy makeshift baseball field is empty when we pass it, surprising for a no-school morning. We keep walking, and I realize the whole town is desolate. Not a car moving down the Big Road. No one going in or out of the Cozy Café, the filling station, the branch library, or the post office, where Mother is working. It's like everyone is afraid another bomb is going to fall.

The only place that looks alive is the Dew Drop Inn around the corner from the grocer. A black van stands outside under the striped awnings, and a smaller black car idles behind it. Their license plates say OFFICIAL. They must belong to the navy men from Whidbey Island, the men who are supposed to find out who did it, the men who won't let Pastor Mitchell bring his wife down from Leonard Creek.

At the grocer, it looks like we're the only customers, but when I get to the dry goods aisle, I see Joey's mother holding the last bag of flour. She clamps it to her chest like it's a baby, her baby. Like she's thanking God that this time she's making the sympathy pie, not receiving it. I don't know whether to interrupt her prayer with a hello.

Willie solves the dilemma for me. "Hi, Mrs. Cooper," he says in a too-loud voice, practically crashing into me.

She lifts her head from her parcel. "Oh, hello, William, Nellie." Her voice is pinched.

"Good morning," I say. Not that there's anything good about it.

"I thought I'd make something for the pastor."

I nod.

"I won't need this whole sack," she says, glancing at the empty spot on the shelf where the flour came from. "I'd be happy to give you . . . I mean, maybe we could . . ."

"How about I give you one of our ration stamps for part of it?" I dig into my pocket for the precious stamp book.

"Well, that would be right nice. Not for something you can't do without, mind you."

I open the book. I need that last red stamp for the butter, so I tear out a blue stamp. She can use it to buy tins of vegetables and fruit.

"Thank you kindly, Nellie. You sure now? You won't get into trouble with your ma?"

"No, our garden is doing fine. We're all right."

She offers me a small smile. "How're you doing today, Nellie? You get any sleep last night?"

"A little. Not really."

"Same with Joey. I heard him up walking around most of the night."

I wish we could've been up walking around together.

"Tell Joey . . ." I start. Tell him what—that I miss him? That he should come over later so we can sit on the stoop and not say a word if we don't feel like it? "Tell Joey I hope he gets some sleep."

"I'll have him bring over the flour later, how's that?"

"That would be fine, thank you, Mrs. Cooper."

After I pay for the butter, Willie and Henry run ahead into Best Novelties. When Ruby and I catch up a few minutes later, I'm relieved to find that it's Mr. Best minding the store and not his wife. If she were here, she'd bend my ear about yesterday. But her husband is hard of hearing, so he doesn't chat much.

That leaves us free to roam the cramped little shop, to pore over the penny candies and magic tricks, the ant farms and the coffin-shaped coin banks. The twins head straight for the shelf of war toys—the assembly-required submarine, the spy pen radio, the tin army tanks, the balsa fighter planes. Ruby and I loiter by the games.

"Y'know what I was thinking about?" Ruby leans against a row of Silly Putty. "I was remembering that time Mrs. Flynn decided to collect our history notebooks. How Dick Patzke turned ten shades of red because he'd filled all the margins with cartoons about her." She smiles to herself. "Why would he do a thing like that?"

"Because he has a big fat crush on her. Had a big fat crush."

"Kinda makes me wish I didn't tease him about it . . . Nellie?"

"Uh-huh?"

"How're we ever gonna face those empty seats when school starts back up?"

I feel overheated all of a sudden, like this cramped little shop just got even smaller and tighter. "I don't think I can. I don't think I can face it."

"Yeah," she says. "I mean, I know they're gone. But when I see those empty chairs, then I'll really know."

She's right. I dread the first day back. And I hate the enemy more than ever, whoever that enemy turns out to be.

Henry comes running down the aisle wielding a toy gun and making banging sounds. I tell him to hush up. He doesn't, just runs to another aisle.

"It should've been Irene Kava, not Joanie." Ruby rocks on her heels. "That twit better not cross us again."

"She probably will," I say. "I kind of tormented her at the salvage drive Saturday."

"She deserves it."

"That's what Joey said. She's sweet on him, you know."

Ruby rolls her eyes. "Tell me he's smart enough to see through those batting eyelashes."

"He's a genius."

The shop door jangles open, but it's just Mr. Best stepping outside for some air. Maybe he's overheated too.

"I hope those navy men hurry up and figure this whole thing out," I say.

"Even if they do, who says they'll tell us?" Ruby asks.

"They have to."

"Gramps says they keep all kinds of things secret."

"Well, this better not be one of them. Let them keep secrets about little green Martians or the Man in the Moon. I want to know who did it, and I want the killers to pay."

Willie appears at my side now, a comic book in one hand and a bird whistle in the other. "I'm hungry."

"Didn't you have breakfast?" I ask.

"Forgot."

I sigh, pull a dime out of my pocket. "Go get something out of the candy case. Two things for each of you. You want anything, Ruby?"

She shakes her head.

"I expect six cents back." I hand Willie the coin, and he runs to find Henry. "This is the five-minute warning," I call after him.

Twenty minutes later, I drag the twins out of the shop. We retrace our steps past the Dew Drop Inn, the post office, the empty makeshift baseball field, and on to Ruby's house, where her grandpa is checking on the birds. Mother does make it home for an early lunch. Then when she heads back out, I doze on the living room sofa while Henry and Willie listen to *The Adventures of the Thin Man* on the wireless.

Sleeping seems like a good way to pass this day, this first day Joan Patzke and the others didn't wake up. This day that dawned over six cold beds, chilled from a night of lying empty. This day that Pastor Mitchell sat at his breakfast table alone. When you sleep, you don't have to think or talk. And I'm bone-tired of thinking and talking.

I wake with a jolt when the front door slaps behind the

twins. *Thin Man* is over, and they're going outside to play. It's a perfect chance to fall back into the nothingness, except that I see something in the foyer. No, not something. Someone. Someone who must have walked into the house as the boys were walking out. I get up.

"Mrs. Cooper?"

"Hello, Nellie." Over her dress, she wears an apron with a pocket shaped like a giant cupcake. She was wearing that same apron, I remember, the day Mother and I brought over the pie, after Peter died. "I hope I'm not disturbing anyone."

"No, but Mother isn't home from the post office yet." Now I see she's holding something under her arm. It's the flour sack.

"That's fine. I just wanted to bring you this." She hands me the sack.

So Joey didn't want to stop by. "Thank you." I can hear the letdown in my voice, dry as an old stick.

"Nellie?"

"Yes, ma'am."

"Can we chat? I won't take but a minute of your time."

"I . . . yes, sure. Would you like to sit?"

"No, no, this is fine." She plays with her apron strings. "How are you holding up today?"

"All right," I say. "How's Joey doing?"

"That's what I wanted to talk to you about."

"Uh . . . Oh."

"You probably don't know this, dear," she says, "but Joey's been having a real hard time these past months since . . . since his brother. Oh, he puts up a good front when he has to. But he barely sleeps. Picks at his food. Doesn't do much of anything at all when he's at home."

I nod and look at my feet.

"Anyway," she goes on, "that may or may not be relevant. The point is, he blames himself for what happened yesterday."

"What?" I look up. "He wasn't even there. He was parking the car."

"Yes, that's what the pastor said. But Joey insists it's all his fault."

"How does he figure that?"

"He says if he hadn't picked a quarrel with the pastor—if they hadn't spent all that time arguing—they'd have gotten back to the others sooner. Says they could've, would've warned them off."

"Ridiculous," I say.

"That's what I told him. Sheer nonsense."

"Mrs. Cooper, it was my idea to go to the creek in the first place—did you know that?"

"Oh, Nellie." She puts her hand on my arm. "It's not your fault either. It's the fault of whoever planted that bomb." Outside, the twins squawk. Somewhere, a clock strikes the hour. Then Mrs. Cooper takes her hand back from my arm. "About this squabble Joey says he had with Pastor Mitchell . . . any idea what it was about?"

"No, ma'am," I lie.

"No, of course not. I'm reaching for straws, is all."

"Do you want me to talk to him?"

She shakes her head. "He hasn't left his room since yesterday."

Poor Joey.

"Anyway, I'd best get back. Thank you, dear, thank you kindly. You take care now."

I thank her for the flour again and tell her to watch the bottom step, which is starting to come loose. But what I'm thinking about is how sorry I feel for Joey. How could he blame himself for this? Does he blame himself for Peter too, for letting him go off to war? I need to sit down and think this over, but before I get halfway back to the sofa, there's a knock at the door. Whoever it is, I don't want to talk.

It's the pastor. Okay, maybe I do want to talk. But I don't, not really. I want both. I want neither.

I open the door. "Pastor Mitchell."

"Hello, Nellie." He steps inside and takes off his hat. "Just wanted to see how you're making out."

I'm probably the one who should be asking how the other one is doing, but I don't because I'm pretty sure I know how he's doing. Terrible. Instead, I let out a breath and make room for him to enter. "Come on in."

He drops himself heavily onto one end of the living room sofa, and I perch on the other end. I notice one of the boys' marbles on the floor, a blue one, back in the corner. I spot a dust bunny under the lamp table.

"Would you like a glass of water or anything?" I ask.

"Thank you." He shakes his head. "So, how are you doing, Nellie? How was your night?"

I try to think of what and how much to say. I want to be truthful, but I don't really feel like sharing. "I'm sad," I say. "And scared." Then I feel horrible for complaining to him.

He tents his hands. "Sad, yes, we're all very sad. But why are you scared?"

"I . . ." There's a lump in my throat, and it makes me cough. "I guess I'm scared there might be more bombs. Scared of the sight we saw, the memory. Scared of going back to school. Scared because I thought Bly was about the safest place in the world, and now it's not. Scared for my pa."

"Peter tells us to cast our fears unto the Lord," he says.

"Oh . . ." I look up at him. He must be talking about Peter from the Bible, not Peter Cooper.

The pastor shifts his weight on the sofa. "Now, Mrs. Roosevelt, she says you get stronger every time you look fear in the face."

"Yes, sir."

"I'll tell you something else, Nellie." He leans forward and lowers his voice. "You're not the only scared one. Your pa? He shook in his boots at the thought of going to war."

"H-he did?" I didn't think Pa was afraid of anything. "Did he tell you so?"

"When he first signed up." The pastor sits back. "Bullets and bombs, that's all he could think about. Bullets and bombs."

"Bombs," I mutter.

"So I asked your pa why he was doing it, why he signed up."

"Why did he?"

"Because he loves his family so much." The pastor rubs his nose. "Because he wants a peaceful world for them. For you. Once he realized that, he wasn't so afraid anymore."

My eyes start to mist, so I brush them with the back of my hand. "Is that why you always say love drives out fear?"

"Ah, so you *have* listened to my sermons."

"Uh-huh." *Some of the time, anyway.* "Pastor?"

"Yes?"

"I'm awful sorry. For you. For Mrs. Mitchell."

"Thank you." He closes his eyes and wets his lips. "It's going to be a long road for me, for us all."

"Yeah." And then I blurt out the question that's been eating me since yesterday. "Aren't you mad, Pastor? Aren't you furious with whoever planted the bomb?" Maybe I shouldn't have said it, but I can't help it. He deserves to be mad. He should be mad . . . shouldn't he?

He opens one eye, then the other. "Mad. That's a big word. Yes, I suppose I am—I'm human, after all." He adjusts his eyeglasses and works his jaw. "But I'm working on it . . . on forgiveness."

"Forgiveness?" I jump half out of my seat. "How can you forgive someone who—"

"I don't know. I don't know if I can." He tents his hands and studies them. "But if I'm going to practice what I preach, I must try to let go of . . . well, of unmerciful thoughts."

"Like getting-even thoughts? Like hating thoughts?" *Like the kinds of thoughts Joey has, and I probably do too?*

"Exactly." He tries to smile, but it flickers out before it ever starts. "You're—"

The twins burst into the house, quibbling about something or other, trying to out-yell each other, so the pastor stands up and puts his hat back on. "I'd best be off," he tells me. "Don't be a stranger now."

"I won't."

"And give your mother my best."

"I will." We walk to the door. "Pastor?"

He has his hand on the doorknob already, but he doesn't turn it. "Yes, Nellie."

"If you're going over to the Coopers next." I fidget with my shirt buttons. "Will you tell Joey . . . will you tell him . . . "

He takes his hand off the door.

"Tell him what Mrs. Roosevelt said. I think he'll like that."

"Good idea." He nods. "You take care now."

He leaves, and I watch him walk across the street. *Tell Joey not to blame himself. Tell him that too, would you, Pastor?*

26

TAMIKO

May 5, 1945

Tonight I hear the rumbling, like the beat of a tsutsumi drum, and I tell myself it's distant thunder. I can't fool myself for long, though. Kure City, so close to us, is being bombed. The only thing I don't know is whether the outlying villages are next. Will the bombs rain down here on Shinji-cho?

I've known many fears, but none like this. It's a sword in my ribs. A boulder on my lungs. A fever in my heart. I'm afraid of burning in the ravenous fires. Of getting crushed under a shattered cottage. Of losing my aunt. Of never seeing Kyo again, or Suki. I'm a cowering insect, cornered by a heavy broom.

"Tamiko, run to the shelters behind your school," Auntie says.

"I wouldn't leave you behind," I say, and my voice tells her I mean it. I only hope Pāru is able to make it there. She shouldn't be alone. No one should be alone tonight.

We turn off the lamps, light a small candle, and lie down under the low table. Meager protection, but it's all we have. I wonder if Suki is doing the same thing with her family or if she made it to the shelters. I haven't seen her these last two days, since our quarrel. I wish I hadn't been so sharp with her. I hope she's all right. I hope she has the spirit to endure this night.

Now we wait. It doesn't take long for the rumbling to turn to screeches, like the sky is cracking open and letting the fury of a thousand angry gods pour out. The bombers are so low in the sky, I think they might land on our rooftop and toss their explosives through our windows by hand. They are terribly, shockingly loud.

My breath stops with every shrill whistle. Each explosion startles me more than the one before it. I wonder if Kyo is afraid too. Kyo, who was all coolness and certainty the day he marched off to war. Kyo, who's out there trying to fight this fearsome enemy, with no roof to protect him, no loving aunt to light him a candle, only a helmet and a gun.

Kyo, if he's even alive.

"Auntie?" I ask, our heads pressed together.

"Yes, Tamiko-chan."

"I hid a Daruma doll in Kyo's rucksack. Do you think he keeps it with him?"

She wiggles a little further under the table. "If I know your brother, he gave it to someone he thinks needs it more than he does."

"Oh . . ."

"And I think this kindness will bring him zenkō. That's the kind of act that always brings good karma."

"Do you really think so?"

"I do."

We can't tell how close the blasts are. Is it the cottage a few streets over, or the one next door? It's all around us, the whole sky stitched with fire, the red threads falling to earth and igniting whatever they touch.

I think of Pāru again, and of Eguchi-sensei with his bride. I think of Grandfather, who used to tell us to beware the onibi— the vicious fireballs that will suck your spirit out if you get too close. Tonight, the onibi that swarm the night skies have American flags on their fiery tongues.

And then it hits me. Suki was right. This night, this attack— it's revenge for the balloon bombs. The balloon bombs that I helped build. It's an eye for an eye. It's rust from the blade. Suki understood this while the Americans were still at a distance. Not me. I couldn't see it until they arrived at our doors. I wish I could run to her and tell her I get it now.

"It's late," Auntie says. "You must try to sleep."

"I can't," I say.

"Only the guilty and the old cannot sleep. You are neither." *Oh, Auntie, if only I could turn back time.* I'd call the balloons home like lost sheep. I'd shear their washi coats before they reach their journey's end. But I can't.

I turn my head to see her. "Aren't you afraid?"

"What good would fear do me?"

"Then you are. Afraid."

She sighs from somewhere deep inside. "Let's close our eyes and dream of morning."

As I lie here with the tabletop above me, I compose my will. Not that I have anything to pass on if I should die tonight, not even a handful of white rice. All I have is a message. Or maybe it's a prayer. Or maybe it's simply desperation.

To anyone who survives this night, please don't judge me too harshly. I thought I was doing the right thing.

To my parents, thank you for your constant presence.

To the kami, please protect Kyo, Auntie, Suki, and all the other living souls. Please call the onibi fires away.

To those who die tonight along with me, I ask your forgiveness.

The dawn breaks so silent, so still, it could be death. Or peace. Or a mischievous house-spirit plugging my ears. No, it's not death. It's morning, and we're still alive. Somehow, we're still alive.

I slide out from under the low table, careful not to wake my aunt, who is snoring lightly. Stretching my stiff legs and walking over to the window, I see a broken spider web pressed against the pane. All that work, all that silk embroidery, ripped to pieces in the bombing. A tooth for a tooth.

I open the front door, and the burnt air immediately attacks my nose and eyes. Tree branches litter the narrow road. Toppled electric lines spark and hiss. There isn't a single living thing about, not a squirrel, not a bird, not a butterfly. By some miracle, though, the houses on our lane are still standing. I look to the sky, darkened by the ashes that swirl and rain down, and wonder what spirits held us through the night, protecting us from onibi. Then I start to walk.

I head west in the direction of Kure City. The closer I get to the city line, the harder the going gets. I walk among broken buildings, some of them still flaming, others smoldering. I tread over melted glass and cracked glass and glass shattered into a hundred million jewels. I slog past people surveying the rubble of their homes, looking for something or someone who may have survived. I wander past a shirtless man whose back is scorched.

I want to tell this man, "I didn't know. I didn't know that this is what bombs do."

He looks up at me as I pass. "That's a lie," his eyes accuse.

"Yes, it's a lie, but it's also the truth."

The man scans the row of charred cottages. You know why this happened to us, he seems to be saying. Don't you?

Yes, I silently admit. It's because my ten thousand floating warriors angered the enemy. So the enemy sent ten thousand warriors of their own. Maybe twenty thousand. Or a million.

The man walks on. I should keep walking too. Suki's street is only a little farther. I should go to her to see if she and her family are all right. But what if they aren't? What if they're . . . ?

I turn around and hurry home.

27

NELLIE

May 7, 1945

Ruby and I sit on the gymnasium bleachers, along with most of the town. In front of us stand the two navy men from Whidbey, the ones who've been here the past day and a half, sleeping at the Dew Drop Inn, going back and forth to Leonard Creek, not answering anyone's questions, telling us not to panic. Now they're ready to talk to us.

One of the officers walks up to the microphone in the middle of the gym floor. He looks stiff in his dark, brass-buttoned uniform with the gold stripes at the cuff. He looks kind of nervous, too. My stomach clenches.

While the officer adjusts the mike, I scan the bleachers. Pastor Mitchell sits front and center, between our teacher, Mrs. Flynn, and someone I don't recognize, maybe a newspaper man from Klamath Falls. Joey isn't here, though. I wonder if he's still holed up in his bedroom, blaming himself. I don't see Mr. Patzke or Mrs. Shoemaker or any of the other parents. They're probably in their bedrooms too, trying to fall into a dream, trying not to think.

There's Mr. Kava on the other side of the gym, standing against the wall. I wonder if he's glad he sent all those boys off to fight whatever enemy did this. Or maybe he regrets it—because no matter how many soldiers he sent overseas, an enemy still came.

"Good morning," the officer at the mike says, his voice assured, his silver hair catching the morning light. "I am Lieutenant Daniel Merrill from the naval air station on Whidbey Island. Please accept my heartfelt condolences for the great tragedy your community has sustained. My colleague, Dr. Philip Overbye, and I are here to answer some of the many questions you certainly have."

"Who was it—the Japs or the Krauts?" calls someone a few rows behind us.

"What're you gonna do about it?" says someone from the other side of the room. Wait, not just someone. It's Ruby's grandpa. He must have walked in when I wasn't looking.

Lieutenant Merrill raises his hand for quiet. He draws a breath and sweeps his gaze over the faces in front of him. "Ladies and gentlemen, the victims died from a bomb sent by a hydrogen balloon from Japan."

Murmurs ripple through the gym like wind through the junipers. Ruby and I clutch hands. So the bomb is from Japan— the country that brought Pa to the Aleutians. I feel sick, the kind of sick where you don't feel like you're in your own body. The kind of sick where it feels too awful to be inside yourself.

The lieutenant continues. "The Japanese have been launching hundreds if not thousands of such balloon bombs since last fall in an attempt to wreak havoc on the Pacific coast of our nation."

Hundreds? Thousands?

"The US military has known about the Japanese air-bomb campaign since November, and we have intercepted several of them," Lieutenant Merrill says. "However, we felt it prudent to keep this information out of the press."

"Prudent?" Mr. Kava roars. "How were those poor picnickers supposed to know there was danger when you kept it a damn secret?"

The mutters rise to shouts. Lieutenant Merrill looks to his colleague, who steps up to the mike.

"Ladies and gentlemen," says the doctor, a younger, dark-haired man who stands a full head taller than the lieutenant. "People!" His steely voice quiets the audience. "There are two reasons we silenced the press on this matter. One, to keep the enemy from finding out that any of the balloons ever made it to America. Two, to avoid terrorizing the whole nation—which, of course, is what our enemy wanted in the first place."

The room erupts. A few people walk out—they've gotten the facts they came for. Ruby's grandpa takes a few steps toward the door, then changes his mind. Everyone else stays, and they all have something they can't wait another second to say. Dr. Overbye lets the mayhem go on for a minute.

"However," the doctor says loudly, loud enough to turn people's attention back to him. "In the wake of the current disaster, we have decided to lift the gag order. The press will now be allowed to report on the balloon bombs, in the hope that future catastrophes will be averted."

"Well, it's a little late for us, isn't it?" says the head of our police, Chief Gifford. He lost his nephew in the blast. "What the hell were you thinking? If you were thinking at all." He gets up and leaves the gym.

No one speaks, not even a whisper. It feels worse than when everyone was clamoring. I want to run out. I want fresh air, but Ruby still has my hand. Now Lieutenant Merrill steps back up to the mike, asking if we have any more questions. Any more questions? Questions are all we do have. Questions and grief and fear. And anger. Lots and lots of anger.

Mr. Best from the novelty shop stands up and asks, "How do you know it was the Japs and not the Krauts or the Italians?"

Lieutenant Merrill nods. He looks a little relieved, like someone finally asked a question he can answer. "We know it was the Japanese," he says, "because last fall we brought in a team of geologists to examine the sand in the balloons' ballast bags. By identifying the crystals and the microbes in the sand, the scientists were able to narrow down the source of the sand—not only to Japan, but to the specific coastal area there."

"What're you doing about it, now that you know?" asks Mrs. Black, who runs the Dew Drop Inn. "How're you gonna make 'em pay?"

"We made them pay by destroying their hydrogen plants," the doctor says. "We're still making them pay—by American B-29 bombers."

Now there's applause. "Taps for the Japs!" a few call out. "Smack 'em down!" Mr. Kava and Ruby's grandpa shake hands. "Death from above!"

Part of me wants to cheer too, but then I think of Pastor

Mitchell working toward forgiveness. I think of the explosion at Leonard Creek, how incredibly loud it was, and I have to ask myself something. If one bomb is that thunderous, what is it like in the Japanese villages and cities, where our own bombs are falling like rain?

Still, these were my friends. This is my town. How can I feel mercy? How can I feel anything but rage? I guess that makes me more like Joey than the pastor. More like all these people clapping their hearts out. I put my hands together and join in.

It takes a moment, but soon the applause changes. It's not just a wall of chaotic sound anymore. It's a rhythm, a beat, as if some invisible conductor is guiding all our hands. Our fierce, determined hands.

I clap harder now, for victory over Japan, a grand slam, a crushing defeat. I clap until my hands hurt, and then I keep on clapping.

28

TAMIKO

May 6, 1945

I barely get back from my bleak walk around the village when a light rap sounds at the door. I open it to find a ghost standing there. No, perhaps not a ghost. Perhaps Pāru. But she's so pale and shrunken, she might as well be one. Then I see the slab of freshwater eel in her hand, and now I'm sure she's a ghost, a ghost with the power to make food magically appear.

"Pāru?"

"Good morning," she says in a voice filled with smothered tears.

"Please come in, Pāru-san."

Now my aunt is here, putting an arm around Pāru and welcoming her in. Pāru seems solid enough, so maybe I'm wrong about the ghost. Or maybe our whole village is in another world, a burned-out, bombed-out world where fresh fish sit next to ashes, where impossible things are possible, where nothing is what you expect.

The eel smells exquisite as Auntie gets it ready on the grill.

Pāru doesn't tell us how she got her hands on it, and we don't ask. We don't want to hear if she snatched it from the rubble of a destroyed home. We don't want to know if she had to trade her ancestors' urns for it. This is not a day for looking back or looking forward. It's a day for sitting together at the table, sharing a meal, and being glad we're alive. My aunt makes tea, and I help Pāru get settled. We eat in silence until the food is gone.

Pāru licks the last morsel off her lips, eyes closed, like she's trying to memorize the novelty of good food. Then she takes a long slurp of tea and announces, "We're going to lose this war."

Auntie sets down her cup. "We've as good as lost it already."

"Good," I say. I've lost my false hopes. Now all I want is peace—peace and Kyo.

"Good?" Pāru looks at me like I'm an eight-headed dragon. "You can't mean that."

I don't look away from her.

"But we're the ones in the right," she goes on.

I shake my head. "Eguchi-sensei says war isn't about who is right, but who is left." Then I turn to my aunt. "The sooner this war ends, the sooner my brother comes home."

The two of them glance at each other, a strange look in their eyes. I know what they're thinking.

"You suppose he's already dead by now," I accuse. They study their teacups.

"Am I right?" I demand, startled by my own rudeness.

"Tamiko-chan," Auntie says, "the bombs, they're everywhere now."

"He's alive." I'm unable to return her gaze. "I feel it. I know it."

"How do you know?" Pāru asks with genuine interest.

"He has a Daruma doll with him."

Pāru nods and wipes her mouth with the back of her hand.

"May his guardian ghosts watch over him."

I close my eyes and send a silent message to Kyo. *Don't be ashamed of surrender. In war, death is the only defeat. Make sure you're the one who is left.*

After walking Pāru to her cottage on the outskirts, I drum up my courage. It's time to go to Suki's house, to see if she's all right. I have to walk all the way across the village to get there, and I dread the sights and sounds. The fire-horse bites and kicks my hip, as if it too is afraid. As if it wants me to go straight home. But that isn't the right thing, so I press on, ignoring the horse's snorts and squeals.

As I go, I pass many broken things, many brokenhearted people. I think of Ko-no-Hana, the blossom princess, who reminds us how delicate earthly life is. So very delicate. Delicate as friendship.

I pray that I'll find Suki safe in her home. If the spirits will grant me that, I'll do anything. I'll even find a way to call back the ten thousand warriors Suki and I helped build. Yes, I'll make ten thousand paper cranes and send them to bring back the balloons before they can hurt anyone else. Ten thousand narrow beaks upon ten thousand curving necks above ten thousand pairs of wings. Ten thousand cranes of peace.

I do my best to stay positive as I walk. Suki's house is well-built, I tell myself. It wouldn't crumble like so many other homes did. Suki's family is always lucky, the luckiest people I know. She can't die after she has worked so hard to get well. That wouldn't make sense. She's getting well so she can live, not so she can perish.

But when I turn onto her street, hope flutters away like a cherry blossom in the wind. Only two houses are standing, and they aren't hers. Everything else is wreckage. Gone. Destroyed.

"Suki," I moan, and then I howl it. "Suki!"

I try not to weep as I race down the street, but I can't help it. Half blind with tears, I creep past toppled walls, smoking futons, shattered room screens, a chair. When I get to Suki's cottage, the only thing I recognize is a sliding door and a laundry pole sticking out from a mound of ashes and glass. Her house is in pieces.

My stomach drops to my feet and lurches up into my chest. I feel sick. Sicker than if I ate a bucket full of still-poisonous acorns. Sicker than I've ever felt.

"Suki!" I hear myself call out again. As if she could hear me. As if she could have survived this.

My bad hip gives out, and I fall to my knees. I cry and cry and cry right here in the middle of the road. I cry for everything I've lost, everything Suki has lost, everything the enemy has stolen. I cry too for the part I played in angering the Americans. I cry until I'm dry. Then I simply sit here, empty as a forgotten corner, cold as a slab of stone.

I'm all alone. Alone because Suki is gone. Alone because maybe Kyo is gone too. He probably is. I was stupid to let myself believe anything else. And now Suki isn't here for me either. No smirky smile, no blanket to share, no arm to lean on, no kind words. I don't know what to do without her. I don't know how.

The next thing I know, a hand touches my shoulder. I jump. Is it Suki's ghost? Is it an American soldier? No, it's a woman in a shift dress with a bandanna around her forehead.

"Are you all right?" she asks.

I point to the rubble. "My friend."

She looks at the demolished house. Squints. Looks back at me. "Suki?" I nod.

"That's a very lucky family," she says. "Yesterday they decided to visit their little boy out in the countryside. Suki's brother—Nori. They're tucked away in the farmlands, safe."

Suki is alive?

Suki is alive! Her whole family is alive! I start to sob all over again. Suki, my sweet Suki, is all right.

"Th-thank you, thank you, obasan," I stammer. No more forgotten corner, no more slab of stone. I'm a person again. Because Suki lives.

The woman reaches out her hand to help me up. I take it, and when I stand, I see the sadness in her face.

"Oh, oh," I say. "Are you . . . Do you live here?"

"My family is lucky as well. Our house stands." She surveys the ruins and sighs. "Next, a rice ball will fly into my mouth."

I wipe my eyes and discover that I'm smiling. "I'm glad for you, obasan," I sniff.

"Thank you." She straightens her bandanna and smooths out her dress. "Would you like to come inside for a bit, take a rest?"

I'm drained, and my fire-horse is still bucking. I desperately would like a rest, but I shake my head. "I must hurry home, thank you. I have many paper cranes to make."

Her eyebrows rise.

I head up the road. "Ten thousand of them!" I call over my shoulder.

At home, I go to my room and take my diary out from under my futon. Not to write. To tear. I sit down, tear out a sheet, and try to remember what my grandmother taught me. Fold, crease, unfold, repeat. The sheet I use, the first page of my diary, is from two years ago. My handwriting was looser then, younger. My words were silly—year of the sheep, year of the monkey, New Year's, Girls' Day—and I have no use for them now.

I make the square base, then do the petal fold. Push, fold, crease. I'm remembering how to do it. It's so much better to fold paper into cranes than to glue paper into warriors.

Now I make the bird base. Unfold, fold, crease. Grandmother said cranes live for a thousand years. Eguchi-sensei says they can live for seventy years. Seventy years—I'd welcome that for Kyo, for Suki, for any of the hundred million shattered jewels. Who needs a thousand?

I make the reverse fold for the head. Crimp, pinch, crease. Then the tail and the wings. My first paper crane is finished. I'll use up my whole diary and still have 9,900 birds left to make.

If only the washi paper didn't all get used up for the balloons. If only. I tear out another sheet from my diary and begin the second crane.

29

NELLIE

May 8, 1945

The caskets stand side by side in front of the church, one for each of them. I wonder which one belongs to Joan, which one to Mrs. Mitchell and her baby. I can't take my eyes off the wooden boxes, lined up so neat and polished, like gifts under the tree. I want to stay out here and watch over my lost friends, the way I did that day on Leonard Creek. But Mother scoots the twins inside, and Ruby pulls my hand, so I move along.

The pews are packed like I've never seen them. The whole town has turned out, I think. It's already sweltering in here, and it's only nine in the morning.

I don't know why, but I feel like everyone is looking at me, like maybe I know something or could have done something. Like, what makes me so special that I get to live and the others don't?

We can't find five seats together, so Ruby and I slip into the row behind Mother and the boys. Joey and his parents are on the far side of the chapel near the windows. Irene Kava and her family are a couple of pews behind them. The first three rows are reserved for the victims' families.

This morning before we left the house, we turned on the radio for the latest out of Klamath Falls. The announcer said that earlier this morning, General Eisenhower received Germany's unconditional surrender. The war in Europe is over. The war in Europe is over, and we're all overjoyed. We just can't feel it.

"Let us begin," Pastor Mitchell says at last. He stands before us in the baking room, but I don't think he's really here, and neither am I. We're both back at Leonard Creek. Maybe Joey is too.

In my mind, we're all there, all nine of us, the way it was supposed to be. The pastor and Joey go to park the car, and the others find a curious thing in the woods, but it's just a rabbit nest. I stay behind to dip my toes in the creek and peek inside the picnic basket. Then we have lunch, do a little fishing, and go home. A simple, forgettable afternoon.

An impossible afternoon.

The pastor's voice is quiet, almost hushed today. It would probably do his heart some good to bellow and rant, but he doesn't. Instead, he reads scripture on forgiveness and healing, saying the words like he means them, like he's really finding some kind of peace in the verses. My eyes slip over to Joey. He looks anything but peaceful. His mouth is as tight as a stretched rubber band, his cheeks are as red as one of Mother's tomatoes, and he keeps rubbing his neck. Poor Joey.

Near the end of the service, the pastor turns over his pulpit to anyone who wants to offer a reflection. Teachers, friends, aunts, uncles, and cousins form a gray line at the altar, trying to bring the dead back to life with their words. I don't go up, but at the last minute, Ruby does.

Her strawberry curls tucked behind her ears, her hands gripping the lectern, she looks out at the chapel. "When Joan Patzke and I were little," she says with a quiver, "we tried to catch the Tooth Fairy. We spent a whole summer making traps. Every time we found out someone lost a tooth, we brought them a trap.

"We never caught the fairy. Not even when our own baby teeth started falling out. I thought we wasted our whole summer. But you know what Joan said?" Ruby swallows her tears down. "She said, 'It's okay. What were we going to do with the Tooth Fairy anyway?' And as soon as she said it, I knew she was right. That's how wise Joan was."

Ruby comes back to me, and we squeeze hands. "You did good," I whisper.

"I don't know why I said any of that," she whispers back. "I had to say something, and that's what came out."

"It was perfect."

"Thanks."

The pastor leads the closing hymn, and it's over. I'm stuck to my seat with sweat. Ruby looks woozy. The whole chapel seems to exhale, as if we were holding our breath the whole time. As if we didn't know whether the pastor would make it through the service. Or whether the parents, brothers, sisters, and grandparents might collapse on the spot. It feels good to breathe again, even if the air is bitter.

Everyone starts filing out of the chapel, spilling into the foyer and onto the front steps, waiting while the pallbearers carry the caskets to the cemetery out back. My belly twists into a pretzel. I've seen a coffin lowered into the ground before, but that was different. It was my grandmother. She was old, and there was only one of her.

"Look," Ruby says.

I follow her gaze. There, in the little hallway by the washrooms, Irene Kava is talking to Joey. She has him cornered, standing too close, touching his arm. He twiddles the knot of his tie like it's too tight, like it's the knot choking him off, not Irene. If only I could hear what she's saying.

"I have to use the lav," I announce.

"Me too," says Ruby.

"No, let me do it. I'll tell you everything. You go find Mother and the twins."

She sighs. "Kick her in the shins for me, will you?"

"Not in church. Maybe later."

I head toward the washrooms, eyes down, pretending I don't see them, hoping they don't notice me, but not really caring if they do. Irene is talking low, but I can hear every word now.

"I've never lost anyone before," she says. "Can you believe? Still have four grandparents and everything."

There's a little pause. I picture Joey squirming, trying to loosen his tie with one hand.

"I never knew what it felt like to have someone die right out from under me," she goes on. "But now . . . now I've lost five friends."

They were never your friends, Irene.

"Five people who've always been in my life—gone," she chitters. "And that's how come I can understand you better now, Joey. I understand how you must feel, losing your poor brother."

I have to bite the inside of my cheeks to keep from bellowing at her. Know how he feels? Irene has no idea how Joey feels, how furious he is, furious enough to start a fire in her shed. And she'll never, ever know how it feels to have your family off at war. She says she understands, says she's all torn up like he is, but it's a trick. She's trying to dupe him into liking her.

I'm at the washroom door now. I can't just stand here, so I go in and use some toilet paper to blow my nose. When I get back to the hallway, they're both gone. I wonder how Joey wriggled away. Unless she followed him outside.

I catch up with Ruby and Mother at the cemetery. The twins, looking uneasy, hang back from the gathering. It looks like a lot of people are skipping this part, going home or off to work or wherever it is they'll pass the rest of this endless day. I see Irene but not Joey—I guess he had to leave if he wanted to shake her loose.

"Well?" Ruby asks.

"Nothing but Irene making batty eyes at Joey."

"Tell me he didn't fall for it."

"I don't think so."

Pastor Mitchell calls us all to attention. He says the farewell prayers, but I don't really hear him. I'm busy saying a silent farewell of my own:

Goodbye, Joan, Dick, Sherman, Eddie, and Jay.

Goodbye, Mrs. Mitchell and your unborn baby.

Goodbye, old, gentle Bly.

Goodbye, other war, the war that was happening somewhere else, somewhere far away.

Goodbye, other Nellie, the one who thought a day like today would never happen, not here, not now, not to me.

It's late afternoon, and even though the funeral was just a few hours ago, it feels far away already. I'm thinking about school starting back up tomorrow, about the empty seats that no one will mention or touch or even look at. How I'll never hear Eddie Engen's impersonation of Mrs. Flynn again. How I never knew Joan had two middle names. How her brother had a birthday coming up this week. I wish the school year could be over already.

Mother decides to take a rest. The boys head outside. As for me, I'm in the kitchen doing the lunch dishes, but my head is off somewhere else. Off to Joey's front step, over to the Aleutian Islands, up to the stars. Anywhere but right here.

Then a voice comes spilling in through the open window, and I come back from my wanderings. The voice outside sounds frantic. I turn off the faucet and listen for the words.

"Water!" It's a woman's voice, coming from the street. "Please, my boy needs water!"

I run to the front door and look out. Sitting on the side of the road, there's a canvas-covered pickup truck, olive drab, marked UNITED STATES. A Japanese woman holding a small child stands next to it, crying for water for her sick son.

I've heard about this, about the army driving the Japanese Americans home from the camps these past few months. This truck must have taken a wrong turn off the Big Road, or else it wouldn't be on a dirt street where no Japanese people have ever lived. Yup, I can see the driver mulling over an oversized map that's draped over the steering wheel.

I guess this woman decided to use the unexpected pit stop to get help for her overheated son. She must have jumped out of the truck bed as soon as the driver came to a stop. Even from here, I can see the little boy's cheeks are cherries.

I peer at the mother and her son, and I start to think. I start remembering what Irene Kava said that day during lunch, how maybe the Japanese Americans are out for revenge. *Go away,* I silently seethe to the woman. Because what if Irene was right? What if the Japanese Americans killed my friends? Or what if they worked with Japan to commit these murders? "Go away and never come back." Because my friends will never come back, not ever.

Almost immediately, I hate myself for thinking this, for thinking it might be true, might possibly be true. Could it be true? No. Mr. Roosevelt said they could all start going home. He said it was okay. And no one's smarter than he was.

I rush back to the kitchen, find a pitcher, and run the tap. As I scramble, I wonder how many people are in that truck and how long they've been in there. Probably a long time, and on such a blistering day.

I bet they're mad about that. I bet they've been mad ever since they had to go away to the camps. Mad enough to . . . ?

I set down the pitcher. Turn off the faucet. Watch the last of the water rush down the drain.

Then I go to the door and look out again. It's just a little boy and his mother. It's the army bringing them home. The army wouldn't free them if there was a chance these folks were against us . . . would they? No, of course not. That's not my enemy out there—that's a family. So like one of the yo-yos at Best Novelties, I bounce back to the kitchen to fill the pitcher and fetch a cup.

As I pick up the brimming pitcher, Mother's voice behind me says, "No."

"What?"

"Don't do it."

"It's just water, Mother. They're thirsty."

"Stay inside, Nellie. Or they'll stone you, too."

"Stone me?" Now I really don't know what she's talking about. With the pitcher still in my hands, I bolt out onto the front steps.

And stop short.

I can't believe what I see. Five neighbors stand a little farther down the road, holding rocks in their fists, staring down the Japanese woman and her son.

One of them is Ruby's grandpa. Ruby's sweet and funny grandpa, who tried to let his doves go free into the world. Another one of them is Mr. Wells, the husband of Mother's friend. Mother's friend, who once dreamed of running off to Hollywood, who now dreams of celebrating the end of the war with a big party. Her two sons are out there too, clutching their rocks.

And one of them is Joey.

My heart sinks so low, I don't think I'll ever get it back. Didn't the pastor tell him about love driving out fear?

Please, not Joey.

I blink a few times so I can see more clearly, so I'll realize this is all a mirage on a sweltering afternoon. But Joey is still there. Joey and Ruby's grandpa and the Wellses.

Could Mother be right? Would they stone me, too? Would Joey stone me? I look at his face, at all their faces, and I can't find the answer to my questions there. They are stony as the weapons in their fists.

Somehow, I see new people too, a circle of flickering on lookers. Joan Patzke is there, no expression on her face except curiosity. Dick and Sherman and Mrs. Mitchell are calmly watching too. I see Joey's brother and Mrs. Flynn's husband, and if I look hard enough I even see Pa. They're all present, but they're distant, removed, like they aren't particularly concerned about which way this will go, like they simply want to witness it. How I wish they'd tell me what to do, but they're mute. I'm on my own here.

"Joey, don't!" I shriek. But my voice is lost over the truck's horn and the driver's shouts of "Get back in the damn vehicle— they're armed!"

Now another boy, he looks around eight or nine, jumps off the back of the army truck and runs to the woman's side. Her son too, I'm guessing. She tries to shoo him back to the truck, but he won't budge. Why won't the truck driver come out and help them?

Ruby's grandpa raises his fist over his shoulder, poised to throw his rock. Joey takes a step forward. So does the Wells family. The woman doesn't move. She's stuck, her eyes fixed, her feet nailed to the road.

If I had a star to wish on, I'd wish for snow. Thick, swirling snow to block my view of those men and boys with the stones. Bracing snow to rouse Joey from his sleepwalk. Crisp snow to cool off the little son, to melt in his mouth and soothe his thirst. Beautiful, noble snow. But no snow is going to rescue us on this hot spring day.

Mr. Wells says something into his older son's ear. Then he takes a slingshot out of his pocket.

"No!" I scream so loud it hurts. "They're just people!" I race down the front steps and across the lawn, with Mother on the stoop yelling, "Stop! Nellie Jane Doud, get back here this instant!"

Half the water has sloshed out of the pitcher by the time I reach the street, but there's enough. I position myself between the Japanese American family and the rock holders. If any of the neighbors is willing to risk hitting me, I'm about to find out.

The woman takes a tentative step forward. I pour water into her cupped hands, and her toddler sips thirstily from it. Her other son takes a drink too, and finally she does. Then they use their wet hands to slick the hair off their foreheads.

"Many thanks," the mother murmurs. "You are kind." She emphasizes the *you* to set me apart from the neighbors. The neighbors who would sooner stone her—or watch it happen— than offer up a cup of tap water.

Before I can say you're welcome, the three of them are running back to the truck and climbing in. As the truck pulls into the road, I see that they are the only passengers left. Which means they had to sit in that broiling rig all day while the other people got off. No wonder they were miserable.

I stand there watching the truck rattle down the road, and I wonder what the littlest boy's name is, where he's been, where he's heading. I wonder where the onlookers went. I wonder so many things at once, I don't even notice the neighbors hurling their weapons, not until I hear the rocks hit the truck's wheels.

"How could you?" I say, barely a whisper.

But Mother is still nearby, and she hears my accusation.

"Folks do strange things when they're upset," she says.

I look into her brown, worried eyes. "I know, but . . ."

"You could have gotten hurt out there." She heads to the stoop and opens the front door. "You really shouldn't have done that."

"No, *they* shouldn't have done it. Shouldn't have thrown the rocks. Shouldn't even have picked them up off the ground."

"Come on inside, Nellie," she says, a scold creeping into her voice. "Before the house fills with flies."

I take a quick glance down the street. Joey is heading back to his house. "I'll come in a minute. I want to see how Joey's doing."

"I said . . . Oh, all right. Don't be long now." The screen door swings shut behind her.

Joey is almost at his driveway when I meet him in the road. He's kicking a stone, maybe one of the stones that hit the army truck, and he doesn't see me until I'm right in front of him.

"Joey . . . " I start, and then I get lost.

"Hey, Nellie," he says. "That was something, huh?"

"Joey, how could you?" I blurt.

"What?" His voice sounds surprised, wounded.

I take a step closer. "Starting a shed fire, okay, fine. But throwing rocks at someone? A little boy and his mother? How could you?"

The hurt on his face turns to something else now. Something hot and red. "How could I do it?" he asks, more hiss than words. "They're Japs, Nellie. The Japs killed our friends, remember? They're our foes. That's how I could do it."

"No, Joey, those people on the truck aren't our enemies. They're Americans. They're practically our neighbors."

He laughs a hard, frigid laugh that freezes my heart. Freezes my heart and makes me ask myself the question I never, ever thought I'd have to ponder: How can I be friends with him now?

I cross my arms. "The Japanese Americans aren't to blame for the bomb, Joey. They're not."

He lifts his chin. "You don't know a thing about this war, do you?"

"I know you've lost more than I have." It's the kindest thing I can think of. It's also the truth. "No one can blame you for feeling bitter about that."

"You don't know the half of it."

"Okay. But Joey, if you're trying to make your brother proud, this isn't the way."

He doesn't say anything. Doesn't try to tell me I'm wrong. Doesn't tell me to stop sticking my nose where it doesn't belong.

I think of the shadowy Peter Cooper who was looking on at Joey. Looking on but most definitely not cheering on. "It's not the way to make your brother proud," I say again. "Don't you see?"

"Nellie." He squeezes his eyes shut. "Oh, never mind. I don't know why I thought you'd understand. You don't understand me at all."

"Then help me understand."

"I can't!" he says so sharply it makes me flinch. "You're just like the pastor with his 'Pick a different path, Joey. Don't pick anger. Pick love, pick goodness. You've got choices, Joey.'"

"Well—"

"Well, he's right," Joey interrupts. "I do have choices. And I choose hate." He turns on his heel and marches up his driveway.

"Joey?"

He gives me a quick glance over his shoulder. "Not now, Nellie."

"Then when?"

But he doesn't hear me. Or he pretends not to.

30

TAMIKO

May 27, 1945

It was easier walking to Kure City this time, now that I wasn't fighting winter winds or trying to hide my limp. Besides, I've been walking on air since we got word this morning that Kyo is safe. Still, by the time I reached the hospital, my fire-horse hip was howling for a rest. When the nurse offered me a chair in the little room at the end of the hall, I fell into it.

Now I sit in this windowless space, my bag on my lap, remembering the Daruma doll I hid in Kyo's rucksack so long ago, how I painted in one eye for his safe return. My greatest wish is to paint in the second eye, once he's home with Auntie and me. Once we're a family again.

I breathe in the scent of medicines mixed with detergent. I listen to the silence of this place. It's so quiet, too quiet. This is where they brought my classmate Keiko after our village was bombed. She didn't make it. Eguchi-sensei didn't even get as far as the hospital.

They didn't say what happened to Kyo, or how he is. The

message only said he was sent here. Which means he's alive! This is the important thing. This is really all that matters. I tell myself that over and over. And yet.

Will I recognize him? Will he recognize me? Will there be anything left of the Kyo I used to know, the Kyo who is my brother? I hear footsteps approaching, and wheels. My heart flutters and bangs.

A nurse pushes his wheelchair in, and I see him before he sees me. Kyo, his face as pale as his white hospital gown. A jagged scar carved into his scalp. An arm in a cast, a foot thickly bandaged. My brother is alive.

"Kyo!" I jump up and run to him, throwing my arms around his bony shoulders.

He puts his good hand on my cheek. "Tamiko," he murmurs, his voice thinner than washi paper.

When I straighten up, the nurse nods to me and retreats from the room.

"You look well," I lie. He looks like a ghost swimming in that white sheet, so colorless that I can almost see through him.

"You look hungry," he says, and I know he's being kind. How I really look is hollow-cheeked and pinched. "How is Auntie?"

"She is . . . she is ten years younger since we got the news that you're all right."

One corner of his mouth turns up, not into a smile exactly, but close enough. "There's a window down the hall. I haven't seen the outdoors in a long time."

"Good idea. The sun is out too."

I throw my bag over my shoulder and wheel Kyo out of the

room. At the far end of the hall, past all the closed doors and medicine carts, we reach a window that overlooks a patch of scrubby grass and a road. The daylight on Kyo's face makes him look a little more solid, a little more real. There's a boy swimming in that white hospital gown now, not a ghost.

I let him take in the view for a few minutes, but then I have to ask, "What happened to you, Kyo?"

He doesn't answer right away. He closes his eyes and lowers his chin, as if he's falling asleep, as if he's dreaming of the front. "I don't know," he says at last. "I don't remember. Which is probably a lucky thing."

I nod. A crow lands on the road, and I watch it peck at something. "And your injuries? How, how . . . ?" I can't get the words out.

"How bad are they? This," he says, raising his casted hand, "this is nothing, just a broken bone. This"—he points to his head—"this is only a cut, some missing hair."

He looks out the window again, but all I can look at is his foot.

"Kyo?"

He lets out a long sigh. "I lost three toes. And shattered my ankle. I'll never walk properly again. I . . . am an invalid, sister."

"I guess that makes two of us."

"Tamiko—"

"A limp isn't the end of the world." I stand up taller. "It didn't keep me from working in the rice paddies last summer, did it? It didn't stop me from walking all the way here today, did it?"

Kyo's eyes dart around the walls, then down to his foot and

up to the ceiling, like he's trying to escape. He's trying to run away, but he can't. He can't even walk yet.

I hold on to the arms of his wheelchair and lean in. "Kyo, I was lucky to live through polio. And you were lucky to live through the war. Don't you see that?"

He finally turns his gaze to me. When he does, his eyes are damp, and it frightens me. Kyo was always the confident one, the calm one, the spirited one. If he isn't my stronghold, then who is?

"Tamiko, I failed you," he says. "You and Auntie and all the hundred million hearts."

"Failed me? You defended me!"

"No, I failed to defend you. Failed to bring victory. Failed to create peace."

My poor, sweet brother. He has risked everything, given everything, and he can't even feel good about it.

I drop my bag into his lap. "I brought you something."

He stares at the bag for a long moment before opening it. Then he reaches in and finds my gift. A garland of paper cranes, the signs of peace. His lips part as he studies it, touching the wings, the beaks, the tails, each bird as white as his ghostly hospital gown.

"Here." I put the garland around his shoulders.

"I don't deserve this," he breathes. "I told you, I did nothing to bring peace."

"You're wrong, Kyo." I adjust the birds so they lie smoothly against his gown. "You brought me great peace when you survived."

"I could have done that from home." He grips the garland.

"I could have stayed right in Shinji-cho and learned how to make origami like you."

"No, you never could have stayed home. Nothing was going to keep you from serving."

He nods and shrugs at the same time.

"And besides," I say. "Making origami wasn't the only thing I did while you were away."

"No? What else?"

I rub my forehead, fold my arms.

"Sister, you're hiding something from me."

Still I say nothing.

"Did you . . . try to bring peace?" he asks.

Now I'm the one looking away. Such a difficult question.

Did I try to bring peace? I wanted to bring peace. I thought I was doing just that. But then Suki helped me see that I may actually have made things worse. So, did I try and fail? Or did I not really try?

He puts his good hand, calloused and raw-boned, on mine. "Tamiko?" he urges.

"It's a long story, Kyo."

"Then you can tell it to me when I get home."

"Yes." I force a smile. "I'll tell you the whole story while you help me make paper cranes."

"But I don't know how to make origami."

"Then I'll have to teach you, the same way I taught Suki."

"Suki makes origami now?" He tilts his head. "I can't picture her having the patience."

"Yes, well . . ." Where to begin about Suki? That sitting is just about all she can do these days, after being so sick? That she and I had a terrible fight, and now that we've talked it out—now that we're best friends again—we do everything together? That since her home got bombed, she's living with us for the time being?

I don't say these things. Instead, I tell him, "I can't get to ten thousand all by myself, after all."

His eyebrows rise. "Ten thousand cranes?"

The nurse appears now, pointing to her wristwatch. "I'm sorry," she says to me. "The doctor is making rounds now."

"I . . . Oh." Our visit is over already. And I came so far to get here.

"You may walk with us, if you like," she offers. "As far as the door to the patient ward."

"Yes, all right."

The nurse turns the wheelchair around and heads down the corridor.

"Ten thousand cranes?" Kyo asks again, holding my hand. "That will take forever."

"That's why you should help us," I say.

"It will still take a long time."

"So maybe you'll be up and walking by the time we're done," I say. "Maybe we'll even have peace by then."

But the truth is, I already have my peace. Because I have Kyo back. I have Kyo and Suki and Auntie, and soon we'll all be together.

The nurse pushes open the door to the patient ward, and Kyo releases my hand. It's time for us to part. We don't say goodbye, though—because this isn't really another farewell. It's more like the beginning of a long hello. The nurse wheels him into the patient ward, and I watch through the small window in the door until they turn a corner.

"Hello, Kyo," I whisper to myself. "Welcome home."

31
NELLIE
May 31, 1945

I'm back at Leonard Creek today, with the pastor. He drives up here on Sundays after church. At first I couldn't understand why, not until I started feeling like I wanted to come too. He said it would be all right.

Traveling up here, just the two of us, his car felt as big and hollow as an empty house. He turned on the radio to fill the space, and we caught Bing Crosby crooning "It Could Happen to You." After that, it was "Stardust" and a bunch of commercials.

"How's Joey doing?" the pastor asked as we turned onto the logging road.

"I . . . I haven't talked to him in a while." Since the day of the funeral, as a matter of fact.

"Maybe I'll ask if he wants to come up here next time. Would he think that's a good idea?"

"Mm . . . I don't know. I don't really know what Joey thinks about anything these days."

He looked into his rearview mirror. "He'll come around, Nellie. Give him some time."

Then "I'll Be Seeing You" came on and I pretended to listen. It felt like such a long ride up there. My legs were actually stiff by the time we parked and got out of the car.

Here we are now, standing on the rim of the hole where the bomb blasted. It's a warm day, breezy, the kind of day that makes you think of picnics in the woods, maybe a little fishing in a creek. All around us the ground is strewn with pine needles, except for the clear spot where the balloon was. The air still smells like fire.

On the other side of the hole, a tree is studded with shrapnel, the sharp metal embedded right into the branches like an odd kind of fruit. The birds in the trees are silent. And if there are cicadas up there, they must be asleep. It's incredibly quiet, even all these days later.

That's the worst thing about being here—the awful quiet. I think I expected to hear picnic noises, fishing noises, normal spring afternoon noises. Maybe I was expecting to find Joan and Sherman here, and Mrs. Mitchell and the others—all of them alive, all of them talking and laughing. But there's nothing here. Nothing but the faint outline of six snow angels. Pretty soon even that will be gone.

"It's peaceful up here, isn't it?" the pastor says.

I nod. Maybe I'll bring Pa up here one day once the war is over. For some peace.

"What made you want to come today?" the pastor asks.

"I don't know. I guess I needed to . . . make sure it really happened. How about you?"

"I'm checking on my lilies."

"Lilies?"

"Come, I'll show you."

He steps down into the hole, right into the hole where Mrs. Mitchell and the others got blown apart. "See here?" He picks up a stick and points to one side of the pit.

I inch closer. "I just see a pile of pine needles."

"This is where I planted two bulbs. From Mrs. Mitchell's garden. They should bloom by late summer, early fall, if they get enough water. I like to make sure they're doing all right."

I squint to see if anything is coming up in this place where six people went down. No green shoots yet. Then I step into the hole with him. It feels like winter down here.

"Why here, Pastor?" I ask. "Why not plant the bulbs at the cemetery, where Mrs. Mitchell is?"

"Good question." He sits on the rim. "Guess I wanted to bring some fresh life to this place. Guess I feel closer to her here. Closer to Winnie, too."

"Winnie?"

He smiles and looks over my shoulder at something far away. "My wife felt she was carrying a girl. We picked out the name Winifred. It means 'peace,' you know."

"That's awful nice, Pastor." I walk to the other side of the hole. "This is where she was, isn't it? Where Mrs. Mitchell was."

He nods. "With her hand resting on her belly. On Winnie."

That's right, now I remember. I jump up on the higher ground with the pastor. "You know what I wonder? I wonder who it was who touched it, touched the bomb and set it off."

"Impossible to know." He scratches his elbow. "But if I had to guess, I'd say it was my Elsye. She was an explorer, that one."

A shiver goes through me, and I have to look away and blink my wet eyes dry.

"You all right, Nellie?" he asks.

"Uh-huh." I try not to sniffle. "Glad I came."

"You're welcome to drive up with me anytime." He stands up. "Anytime you like."

We start walking back to the car, past the big-leaf maples and the ponderosa pines. Underfoot, some baby blue eyes and another purplish flower freckle the way. I try to picture a day when the snow angels' outlines will be gone. When the icy blade in my heart will dissolve. Those saplings over there will probably be halfway to the sky by then.

I get a surprise when the pastor pulls into my driveway after visiting the creek. Joey is sitting on my front steps. I haven't talked to him, have hardly laid eyes on him, since the day the army truck stopped on our street. Has he been waiting for me?

I step out of the car. "Thanks for taking me, Pastor."

"Thanks for coming along. Looks like you have some company." He waves to Joey.

"I . . . yeah."

"Well, I'll be seeing you." He shifts the car into reverse. "Let me know if you ever want to do it again."

"I will." I watch him back out of the driveway, then I turn to Joey. "Hi."

"Hi." He's wearing the same black turtleneck he had on the night he lit the fire in the Kavas' shed. As if he's cold. Or in mourning. "Do you have a minute?"

I walk over and sit next to him on the steps—not right next to him, though. I don't think I really know him anymore. And I have a feeling I'm not going to like what he has to say.

"How's the pastor?" Joey looks out to the street, or maybe to his house, anywhere but at me.

"He's all right, I guess."

"And you?" He rubs his chin. "How are, you know . . . how are you?"

His question is too big. There are too many answers. "All right. I guess."

He nods, his gaze still planted somewhere else.

"What about you?" I ask.

"Me?" He shrugs. "I'm okay. Wait, no." Finally he turns his silvery eyes on me. They are ablaze. "No, I'm not okay."

I can't tell if he's angry or sad or maybe even a little crazed. I look away from his glare.

"Don't be afraid of me, Nell," he says, his voice softer. "I'm not gonna hurt you. You or anyone else. I just wanted to tell you, well, you said something that got me thinking."

I run through everything I've ever said to Joey. I've said a lot of things to him. What was it that made him think?

He leans back against the steps. "You told me if I'm trying to make my brother proud, this isn't the way. So I got to thinking, maybe you're right, maybe there is another way." He doesn't say anything else after that, just jiggles one foot against the other.

"Okay, so what's the way?" I shade my eyes with my hands. "How are you going to make Peter proud?"

"That's just the thing." He taps his heel against the riser. "What I figured out is, my brother isn't the one I want to make proud." He wets his lips, swallows hard. "You are."

A swarm of fireflies swoops through my chest. "Me?" I breathe.

"Yup. I'm aiming for the top."

I have to grip my knees because they're shaking. Joey puts his hand over mine.

"That was a rotten thing I did with, you know, the stones," he says.

"Yeah," I answer. "It was a rotten thing all you fellows did. And Ruby told her own grandpa so. Told him he has no business calling his birds damn fools, because that's exactly what he is."

His mouth forms a little smile. Then his face goes solemn. "I'm sorry, Nell. Sorry I threw that stone. Sorry I didn't listen when you said not to. Sorry I got sore at you."

This sounds an awful lot like the old Joey, my Joey, my best friend. Is he back? Suddenly, I realize he's sort of holding my hand.

"Anyway, I wanted to tell you this now because, well, I won't be able to later." He drops his chin. "We're moving away."

"W-what?" No, no, no! It can't be. Now that he's finally come back to me, he can't turn around and leave me again. He can't.

"We're going to California to take over my grandparents' farm. My uncle is coming too."

"But . . ." I have to turn my head away. "When?"

"Next week."

I nod to let him know I heard him. He grips my hand a little tighter, and I squeeze back. "That sounds . . . You must be excited."

"I didn't want to leave without telling you," he says. "I didn't want you spending the rest of your life thinking I'm a crumb. I want you to know I'm gonna spend the rest of my life trying to make you proud."

I press my eyes shut. "How will I know? How will I know if you're making me proud?"

"I'll write you, how's that? Let you know what I'm up to." His thumb skims the back of my hand. "And you. You'll write me back, won't you?"

I open my eyes and try to smile. " 'Course I will."

"I'm counting on it, so you better." He looks at me for a long minute, his eyes shining. Then he leans over and kisses my cheek. "Bye, Nellie."

"Bye, Joey." I don't want to, but I release his hand so he can get going, so he can be where he needs to be.

Joey stands up, blinking something away. Then he hops down the porch steps and heads to the road. Halfway there, he turns around and waves, squinting against the afternoon sun. I wave back while the first tear trickles down my cheek, right past the spot where Joey kissed me goodbye. Then he crosses the road and disappears into his house.

Goodbye, Joey.

If I could fly, I'd wing off to California to be with him. On the way, I'd go to that thirsty little boy and see if he's feeling better. Then over to the theater in Beatty to lose myself in a scary movie for a couple of hours. Or maybe I'd stay right here, just like those silly doves, because this is where Pa will be returning, where Ruby is, and Mother, and even the annoying twins. This is where I first knew Joey Cooper.

After a while, I decide to check the mailbox for a letter from Pa, then remember it's Sunday. Well, we got a note from him a few days ago, so I'm pretty sure he's all right. I stretch out my legs on the steps. I could sit out here all afternoon, just thinking, hoping, imagining. But I have a friend up the road who needs help with her homework, and I still haven't done the lunch dishes, and besides, there's always tonight for sitting outdoors.

I stand up, wipe the dust off my trousers, and head inside to find my geography lesson. And some letter-writing paper, too.

EXPLORING THE HISTORY WITHIN THE BOOK

BASED ON TRUE HISTORICAL EVENTS

The Sky We Shared is based on real events in the United States and Japan during World War II. Most of the novel's activity takes place in early 1945, a few months before the end of the largest and bloodiest war in global history. In Europe during this period, the Allies completed their victory in Europe, including the liberation of the Nazi concentration camps Auschwitz, Bergen-Belsen, Buchenwald, and Dachau. On April 30, Hitler committed suicide in his Berlin bunker, and, a few days later, Germany surrendered, ending the war in Europe. In the United States, meanwhile, more than 120,000 people of Japanese descent who'd been sequestered in internment camps since 1942 were returning home to rebuild their lives.

During this time, Japan fought on against the Allies, despite mounting losses of life and property. In a final attempt to reverse the tide of the war and avenge US air raids, the Japanese Imperial

Forces launched a top-secret offensive in late 1944 and early 1945. That offensive, dubbed Project Fu-Go ("wind-ship weapons") in Japan, is the inspiration for this novel, which tells the Fu-Go story through the eyes of the young people who were caught up in it.

PROJECT FU-GO

The Japanese military built and launched about 9,000 air bombs, or Fu-Go, between November 1944 and April 1945. Each Fu-Go consisted of a large handmade balloon, to which a firebomb was attached. The balloons were partially built by teenage girls, who were an available, nimble-fingered labor source. Seventy feet tall, thirty-three feet in diameter, and made of paper, the balloons were designed to travel above the Pacific Ocean on the high-altitude air current known as the jet stream and then release their payload when they reached the United States. The contraptions would burst into flames upon detonation and were intended to start forest fires, destroy buildings, and kill.

Each hydrogen-filled balloon had to carry 1,000 pounds of gear—including the bomb, ballast, and control devices—across the Pacific Ocean. Thanks to errors in the Japanese wind charts, which underestimated the average time required for the balloons to carry their heavy loads (sixty-five hours versus ninety-six hours), most of the balloons fell harmlessly into the sea before reaching the American mainland. Still, as many as a thousand balloons completed the 5,000-mile trip to the Americas. Most of these firebombs caused little or no damage, due in part to a wet 1944–45 winter that doused the flames. However, there was one fatal firebomb explosion, which took six lives in the small town of Bly, Oregon.

On May 5, 1945, the Bly pastor Archie Mitchell and his pregnant wife took five youngsters to nearby Gearhart Mountain for a picnic and fishing. While the reverend looked for a place to park his car, the others took a hike through the woods. There they discovered what looked like a large deflated balloon. They didn't know a bomb was attached to it, so they ventured closer. As soon as they touched the contraption, the bomb exploded, instantly killing the five children and Mrs. Mitchell. In this way, the victims became the only World War II fatalities in the continental United States. They were twenty-six-year-old Elsye Mitchell; eleven-year-old Sherman Shoemaker; thirteen-year-olds Edward Engen, Jay Gifford, and Joan Patzke; and fourteen-year-old Dick Patzke.

The US government knew about the firebombs before the Oregon catastrophe happened but had placed a gag order on the media to keep Japan from learning what, if any, effect their offensive was having. That was why the young picnickers weren't suspicious about the curious balloon they found in the woods. Thankfully, wartime rationing prevented Reverend Mitchell from using a bus for his outing, or else more children would have come along on that fateful day. The government lifted the press blackout in the wake of the Bly explosion.

FU-GO'S AFTERMATH

While US officials learned about the firebombs as soon as they started to land, they didn't immediately know what country had sent them. To answer that question, the government had to turn to geologists. By examining the sand inside the balloons' ballast bags for minerals and organisms, the scientists were able to trace the contents to northeastern coastal Japan. Using that information, the American military located two of the three Japanese factories that were producing the hydrogen needed to fill the balloons. The US Air Force then destroyed the factories, putting an end to the balloon bomb program.

In 1950, a stone memorial was erected at the site of the Oregon explosion. Since then, a number of Japanese nationals have visited the site, either in person or in spirit, to offer their apologies to the community. For instance, in 1976, Sakyo Adachi, one of the Japanese scientists involved in the firebomb project, visited the memorial and laid a wreath on the monument. In 1987, a group of former Japanese schoolgirls who had been taken from their homes and forced to make the balloons sent personal letters of apology to the people of Bly. They also sent a thousand hand-folded paper cranes—the Japanese symbol of peace and healing—as well as six cherry trees. In 1991, Japanese schoolchildren at the Fukuga Elementary School sent another thousand paper cranes to their sister school in Bly.

To date, there have been 285 confirmed landings/sightings over the years, mostly on the western seaboard from Alaska to Mexico, but some as far inland as Texas, Wyoming, and Michigan. The latest discovery was in 2014, when a balloon bomb was found in British Columbia and detonated by the Royal Canadian Navy. No one knows if more bombs will be identified or whether they will still be live.

NAMES OF THE CHARACTERS
To honor the memory of the Bly victims and the pastor, this book uses their real names, even though their conversations and some of their backstories have been fictionalized.

MORE WWII HISTORY

TIME FRAME FOR *THE SKY WE SHARED*

One might wonder why a story that takes place in the western United States during World War II doesn't have more about the Japanese American internment camps . . . or why a story that takes place in Japan during the war doesn't include the atomic bombing of Hiroshima and Nagasaki. The answer is that *The Sky We Shared* takes place in between these major chapters of the war. When *The Sky We Shared* opens, the internment camps are already closing, and the internees are beginning to return home. When *The Sky We Shared* closes, the Hiroshima and Nagasaki bombings are still three months away. Permit me, then, to include a brief note here on these two momentous subjects:

THE JAPANESE INTERNMENT CAMPS

From 1942 to 1945, the US government forced people of Japanese descent to live in isolated camps. That was more than 120,000 Japanese Americans—more than half of them children—living behind barbed wire. There were a total of ten camps in California, Arizona, Wyoming, Colorado, Utah, and Arkansas.

Established in response to Pearl Harbor and the war, the Japanese internment camps are remembered as a grave violation of American civil rights. As one internee said, "There's not a more lonely feeling than to be banished by my own country. There's no place to go."

THE ATOMIC BOMBS

To hasten the end of the war, President Harry Truman ordered the bombs to be dropped on the cities of Hiroshima and Nagasaki in August 1945. The incredible devastation did lead to Japan's unconditional surrender. Casualty figures are hard to estimate, but even a conservative estimate puts the death toll at well over 100,000—mostly civilians.

Do you think the United States was justified in dropping the bombs? In case you're wondering what other people think, a survey conducted by the Pew Research Center in 2015 showed that 56 percent of Americans at that time approved of Truman's decision, compared to 85 percent in a 1945 Gallup poll. The 2015 survey found that 14 percent of Japanese felt the bombing was justified.

WWII PROPAGANDA

You probably noticed the slogans, posters, murals, and other war-related messages that the characters in both countries encountered. In fact, both the United States and Japan ran active propaganda campaigns to ramp up public support for the war effort. Governments and the media in each country worked to whip up patriotism, engender hate for the enemy, and encourage citizens to cooperate with conservation/rationing, war production, and other activities. Movies, radio programs, books, advertisements, even cartoons carried propaganda messages.

Sadly, many of those messages were racist in nature. The home nation was always portrayed as civilized and moral, while the enemy nation was depicted as subhuman or barbaric. It was often difficult for people to distinguish fact from fiction (or exaggeration) in these campaigns.

Some questions for readers to think about: Was there anything the characters in *The Sky We Shared* could have done differently in response to the racist propaganda? How do you think you would have reacted in a similar situation? Can you identify any propaganda-like messages that you are exposed to in your own environment? How might you verify the "facts" in these messages?

WRITING CROSS-CULTURALLY AND HISTORICALLY

Readers may wonder about my process for determining how the characters in Japan would have lived—what information they would have received, and how they may have felt about various messages they heard or saw. Indeed, research was a large part of this project. For example, I studied firsthand accounts of the Japanese war experience, read books and articles (lots), and immersed myself in (translations of) the popular Japanese media of the day. During my historical and cultural research, I worked especially close with the following people:

MIKIO TAJIMA

Mikio grew up in Japan during World War II. He was born in 1934 in Nishinomiya (outside of Osaka) and was raised there except for his evacuation to the Japanese country-side during the second half of the war. His mother died during a bombing raid. Mikio moved to the United States in 1953 to go to UCLA. From there, he went to Columbia University, where he earned a master's degree in international affairs. Mikio spent his whole career working for the United Nations, advancing his way up to Undersecretary General for Trade and Development.

MICHELE AND TOMOHIRO FUJII

At the time she assisted my research, Michele was a graduate student in the East Asian Languages and Cultures Department at the University of Massachusetts–Amherst. She had been the Japanese editor for two years at Cheng & Tsui Co. in Boston, where she worked on the revised Adventures in Japanese high school textbook series. She now works in the Division of International Affairs at Kansai University in Osaka, Japan. Michele's husband, Tomohiro, was born and raised in Japan and graduated from Kansai University.

PAULA LONG

A school librarian, Paula lived in Japan as a high school student, a university student, and a working adult and parent. In reviewing my manuscript, she consulted with her former Japanese host parents, who were growing up in Japan in the 1940s.

ADDITIONAL READERS

In addition to this research and guidance, I received notes from Japanese American readers of different ages and incorporated their feedback into the edits. This was especially helpful in deepening my understanding of the nuances of how the characters would address one another within Japanese culture.

GLOSSARY

Amaterasu: the sun goddess of the Japanese Shinto religion.

ballast: heavy material such as sand that can be used to stabilize a balloon.

Burma: the former name of the Asian country Myanmar.

cicada: a type of insect. The males make a loud buzzing sound.

gibbous moon: the moon when it appears less than full but greater than a half-circle.

haiku: a poem with seventeen syllables: five in the first line, seven in the second, and five in the third. Haikus often focus on images of nature. They originated in Japan.

kami: not easily translated into English, *kami* is a word for spirits, powers, forces of nature, and ancestors that are worshipped in the Japanese Shinto religion.

kamidana: a miniature home shrine for Shinto kami.

maneki–neko cat: a popular Japanese figurine of a cat waving its paw, believed to bring good luck.

megaphone: a hand-held cone-shaped instrument that amplifies a speaker's voice.

obasan: Japanese term for aunt or older woman.

okaasan: Japanese for "mother."

otoosan: Japanese for "father."

Pearl Harbor: the Hawaiian site of a US naval base that Japan surprise-attacked on December 7, 1941. The United States declared war on Japan the next day.

polio: an infectious and potentially crippling disease. Polio vaccines were first developed in the 1950s and 1960s.

rationing: during World War II, the US government controlled people's access to scarce items, including certain foods.

sake: Japanese rice wine.

salvage drive: a regularly held event where Americans collected materials such as metal scraps and rubber that were needed for the war effort.

samurai: a member of a powerful military class in pre-modern Japan.

Sasquatch: another term for the mythical Bigfoot.

tamagoyaki: Japanese omelet roll.

tatami mat: a type of mat used as a traditional Japanese floor covering.

tsutsumi drum: a traditional Japanese musical instrument, shaped like an hourglass.

tuberculosis: an infectious disease affecting the lungs.

VFW: Veterans of Foreign War, a large service organization for war veterans.

ABOUT THE AUTHOR

Shirley Reva Vernick is an award winning author and journalist. Her previous works include *The Blood Lie*, *Remember Dippy*, and *The Black Butterfly*. Her interviews and feature articles have appeared in numerous magazines, national newspapers, and university publications. She also runs a popular storytelling website, storybee.org, which is used in schools, libraries, hospitals, and homes all over the world. Shirley graduated from Cornell University and is an alumna of the Radcliffe Writing Seminars. She lives in Amherst, Massachusetts.

ACKNOWLEDGMENTS

My deepest thanks to the village it took to create this book, including: the Tajima family (Mikio, Esther and Mark), Michele and Tomohiro Fujii, Paula Long, Liam Saito, May Saito, Liana Penny, Cinco Puntos Press, and Jessica Powers. I'm incredibly grateful to editor extraordinaire Elise McMullen-Ciotti and the entire Lee & Low Books team.

OTHER BOOKS BY SHIRLEY REVA VERNICK

REMEMBER DIPPY

"An enjoyable and provocative exploration
of the clash between 'normal' and 'different'
and how similar the two really are."

—*Kirkus Reviews*

THE BLACK BUTTERFLY

"A hauntingly delicious mix of ghostly adventures, budding romance, and page-turning intrigue that will have you breathless up until the end."
—Marley Gibson, author of the Ghost Huntress series

THE BLOOD LIE

"A powerful—and poignant—reminder
that no person can live freely until
all people can live freely."

—Lauren Myracle, author of *Shine*

RESOURCES FOR EDUCATORS

Visit our website, leeandlow.com, for a complete Teacher's Guide for *The Sky We Shared* as well as discussion questions, author interviews, and more!

Our **Teacher's Guides** are developed by professional educators and offer extensive teaching ideas, curricular connections, and activities that can be adapted to many different educational settings.

How Lee & Low Books Supports Educators:

Lee & Low Books is the largest children's book publisher in the country focused exclusively on diverse books. We publish award-winning books for beginning readers through young adults, along with free, high-quality educational resources to support our titles.

Browse our website to discover Teacher's Guides for 600+ books along with book trailers, interviews, and more.

We are honored to support educators in preparing the next generation of readers, thinkers, and global citizens.

LEE & LOW BOOKS
ABOUT EVERYONE • FOR EVERYONE